IMANI'S HEART

IMANI'S HEART

Book One in the Tiwa Series

JOYIA MANÓN

Queen Suite Print

This book is dedicated to Kid and Papa. The pieces of my heart that extend outside of my body. Thank you for choosing me.

I

NOW

The darkness is his canvas. He imagines the room as it was years ago. This is how he passes time. Seeing in his mind's eye the table on the wall to the right of him. Following the pipes that run through the walls and out of the room. Envisioning the circle of salt that surrounds him. The vent in the corner of the room where a small ray of light sometimes appears, offering him a smaller amount of hope in the darkness. Even less often, sounds trickle into the room from the vent. Too much time has passed for him to stay interested in trying to identify the sounds. He hasn't stopped enjoying them, though. They've kept him grounded in reality. In his reality.

Today, he twiddles with the rope. Once he freed his arms from the chair a long time ago, the ropes became a useful way to pass time. Sitting, standing, twirling, playing with the ropes. Now fully accepting his choices are limited, he is grateful he has them. He'd add an occasional stretch with the ropes to change things up. Not too often. The circle didn't extend him a lot of room and it was another futile task that didn't make sense given his current predicament. Like eating.

Time provided his emotions stability. Hostility, revenge, anger, and rage fed him in the early days. He swung his arms and kicked his legs, cursing his jailer. But edging too close to the circle and being burnt from the inside of his body encouraged him to remain calm. He worked on peace and teetered towards acceptance. He still has bad days.

The newest part of the wall serves as a mental projector screen. On bad days, he hung on to the sliver of light and imagined what his prison used to look like- prior to the wall, prior to the treachery, prior to his living death. He'd remind himself of everything that he built and all that was taken from him. He sat deep in his pain on bad days, careful to not start up swinging and kicking. On good days, he'd get enough sound and light from the vent that he felt more alive than dead. He remembered when he commanded respect from everyone in the room, just by simply walking into it. When his name was on the tongue of every townsperson. He was even known on the mainland. On good days, he could actually form a smile as he recounted his memories.

Today is a bad day. He twiddles with the rope, wishing it were longer. Or stronger. Or one of the dishes he served at his infamous dinner parties. No. None of those would serve the purposes intended. He is unable to die or eat. How long has it been? How many years has he spent in this darkness? In this silence? Withering away slower than he would have if he'd been dead and in a coffin. He speaks aloud to himself. Today is a very bad day. It is a day he recreates conversations long concluded. Righting wrongs he now understands were his grave mistakes. Acknowledging the role he played in his current situation. These are days filled with acceptance and longing. Passing the time wishing he could demonstrate his changed behavior. Stuck in a sleepless dream of how things will never be. He holds on to the rope, fulfilled with the knowledge that his ancestors hear him. They understand that he is sorry. Truly. They hear him and know he means it when he says that if could do it all over again, he would have done it all differently.

He languishes and imagines and apologizes. All in the darkness.

2

Monday

The shops were empty. All of the homes we passed, tidy and tucked away, seemed quiet. Unoccupied. The sun was kinder today than it had been most days of our journey. Clouds provided us blankets of shade at random intervals. Trees shivered with a slight breeze. Large banners that read "Ibeji Village Festival of the Family" surrounded the grassy knoll located in the center of town, rippled with the same shiver. I was still trying to grasp that we were here, in Ibeji Village. In Tiwa.

It seemed like all the townspeople were here. Some formed an animated circle around the official festival dancers. The men, women, and children clothed in purple, yellow, and red performed the Dance of the Family. They battled the rhythm of the drummers with the motion of their bodies. Their clothing, tasseled and layered, spun in colorful circles as the dancers honored the spirits of Ibeji Village with their bodies and spirits. The few folks that weren't dancing were spread about eating, checking out exhibits, or catching up with each other. Goats, chickens, dogs, cats, a few monkeys, and pigs wandered throughout the crowds. Some stayed close to their owners. Others explored as if they were also catching up with each other. I could barely take it all in.

I felt the freedom surging throughout my body. The rhythm of the drums pulled my feet to their staccato beat. I swayed, bent over slightly at my hips, and stomped to the drummer's hands. Right, leftrightleft, right, leftrightleft. My braids twirled and hit my waist, in tune with my body. My white dress, the traditional celebratory clothing of Tiwa, shrouded me in comfort. I held one side of my dress up with one hand and grabbed Mom's hand with the other. We joined the other dancers in their trancelike state. Mom returned my smile as we let the music conceal the unspoken truths and uncovered secrets. My Tiwa heritage and her nondisclosure burned at the back of my mind.

I noticed the young man and his dog standing at a distance from us and the other dancers. He was ok. Attractive, if you liked that tall, basketball-player type. I couldn't help but notice his mahogany skin, flawless from his face to his exposed shoulders and arms down to his muscular legs. Okay- he was beautiful. The large, black dog sitting next to him wagged its tail nearly to the beat. They turned their heads in unison towards me. My head spun so fast back to Mom.

The rainbows of tassels and layers slowed down with the music, the dim of the colors nearly sedating me. The drumming ceased and a voice made an announcement over the speakers about a quick break for performers.

"Mom," I whined as she drew me into a long embrace. Of course she was ignoring the people that herded around us towards other parts of the festival. I gave in. I relaxed into the hug. I could feel the shape of ease that had filled her body over the last couple years. I accepted the affection for what it was. A silent agreement to not talk about the uncomfortable. My body drooped as I leaned into her. This was okay...for now.

The young man gave a hand gesture to his dog. The dog's body softened onto the ground. Its head lolled onto its paws. Its owner smiled and waved, catching me again.

"Hungry?" Mom pulled away and held me by the shoulders.

"Yes!" I wiped a bead of sweat from traveling down my face and avoided the man's direction. The smell wafting from somewhere close by reminded me I hadn't eaten since arriving in Ibeji Village earlier in the day. Mom was always good about reminding me to eat. She was always right. She was right about the move improving my mood. She was right about stopping at the festival before settling down in the new apartment. She was right about how much I would learn about the town at the festival. Maybe I'd find out she was right for not telling me we were from Tiwa.

"Great," Mom said as she gently pulled my arm in the direction of food. I wasn't the five-year-old who used to squirm and try to run all around the streets of Chicago. I am nineteen now, almost twenty. I let her hold onto me anyway. She gave me a quick squeeze. "I want you to try the pounded yam at one of the food stands I saw."

Nearly a head taller than her, I kept careful to stay in step. I was actually enjoying myself. It'd been a while since we'd hung out together, held hands, or been intentional to stay close to each other. Never leaving my room hadn't helped. I realized how much I needed this. After everything. After...

I gently swung our arms and pushed away the questions that nagged me. Why Mom never told me she was from Tiwa. She had never so much as mentioned it. Not even when I was reading voraciously about the land growing up. Thinking about the magic was a good distraction.

When we had passed the other towns and cities in Tiwa, like Ina Village and Iwosan Lake, I knew I had to catch up quickly. Mom had told me about some of the different rituals in each of the towns. How the magic had to be honored to maintain their abundance and safety. I didn't know anything about the Tiwan traditions, especially Ibeji Village. Or "the I.V." That's how Mom referred to it. It all held a familiarity to her. One I wanted to know. I was ready to learn how I could play a part in the daily rituals that helped protect Tiwa. I couldn't wait to make Magic a part of my daily life. My heart skipped a beat. I was eager to learn. The food was a good start.

The pungency of familiar and unfamiliar scents brought me back to the present. I peeked into all the food stands, trying to see what looked good. Or familiar. Helpers in the same uniform cooked, took orders, and served gleefully as the crowds from the festival started to build. Outdoor menu displays described fusions of West African and United

States cuisines. Either I was starving or this food smelled heavenly. Probably a little bit of both. I settled into the dining stand menu that Mom stopped at. By the time I'd read all the descriptions of the dishes, she'd already ordered and gotten the food. She placed some in front of my face.

I eyeballed the white balls held in the paper tray and held them up to my nose. "Mmmmm...I'm not even thinking about Harold's Chicken right now."

Mom giggled. "Pounded yam is usually served with soup. I saw another stand closer to the tables over there that sold some okra soup. Want some?"

"I sure do," I said and followed her. She chose a shady spot under a large oak tree. I watched a large crimson bird whistling in the branches above me while she got the soup. Maybe it was another familiar. Not surprising to me at all, the okay-looking boy and his dog sat one table down from us.

Mom must not have noticed him watching us, otherwise she would have checked in with me to make sure I was okay. She didn't do as much as she used to. After *it* first happened. I didn't mind as much as I used to either. The boy pulled a leash from his pocket and put it on his dog's collar. I smirked when the dog cocked its head. It was like the dog wasn't used to ever being on a leash.

"It feels good to be home," Mom said between bites.

"How long has it been?" I recognized the opportunity but treaded lightly.

But she just focused on the food and the festival. I knew she was avoiding my stare. She finished chewing the food in her mouth and searched the crowd. She must've noticed that boy and his dog.

"I wonder if that's his familiar," she said. I followed her gaze and saw the dude smiling at us. He waved before I could warn Mom to stop staring.

"Did you just return from the mainland?" he called out above the din of the crowd. The drummers were starting their next set.

I took her napkin to slowly wipe the remnants of the pounded yam and soup from my fingers. I'd save the wet nap for when this man left us alone. I studied him, then his dog a little longer. Instead of getting anxious, like I used to, I breathed through it. He was really handsome and he did look about my age. Another lifetime ago, I might have tried my flirtatious smile on him. That part of me wasn't there anymore.

"What?!" I replied to him. My face was drawn into a frown. I knew I sounded like I was cursing. Mom cocked her head at the sound of my voice. I waved my arms, motioning to all the festival noise surrounding us.

The boy stalled. He seemed like the type who didn't know how to react when someone was irritated by his presence. Hmph. He moved to the table between us, posturing for forgiveness. His dog followed on leash reluctantly. Was it bowing too? "I'm sorry," the boy said. "Ba wo ni?" He must've realized he'd forgotten to formally greet us, since we were strangers. Something else in our new home I would have to learn and remember.

"Bawo," Mom replied before I had my opportunity to be rude again. I didn't expect her to scold me for it. She knew it was a defense mechanism for me. "Actually, we are moving from the mainland. To stay in the I.V.," she said.

"Oh," he replied. The table leaned into the soft ground a bit when he scooted closer to us. His dog sniffed where the table leg left a slight indentation. "I haven't seen you before. But you gotta be from the I.V. when you refer to it like that."

My mom smiled gently. I knew she felt me getting more uncomfortable the closer he got to us, the more he spoke. She grazed my hand with hers. I lowered my head and focused intently on the food trapped in my fingernails and cleaned them with the wet nap. From my peripheral, I could see Mom only nod in reply to the dude. That was her way of discouraging any follow-up questions. She knew I was uncomfortable with his closeness. Also, he was unintentionally starting a conversation she wasn't ready to have with me.

"I haven't seen you before," he said again. "How long have you been back?" He must've really been used to being the center of attention.

How could he not read the signs? He was almost standing, ready to get closer.

"We just got back. What's your name, young man?"

Mom. "Shouldn't we get going?" I balled up and tossed the dirtied napkin into her paper tray.

"I'm Teddy," he said, putting his fist out to me.

"Imani." My voice was soft and I avoided eye contact. I only tapped his fist with mine because of the look on Mom's face.

"And your sister?" Teddy reached over to Mom with his fist.

She snickered at his obvious attempt to flatter her. "I'm Imani's mother, Brena," she replied, also meeting his fist with hers. I took that time to fully inspect him. A sheepish grin spread between his chiseled cheekbones. His shiny white teeth were set beautifully against his dark brown skin. He really was handsome.

Mom got up and headed to the recycling bins nearby. "It was nice meeting you, Teddy. Maybe we'll run into you again sometime." Finally. Escape.

I got up and walked backwards, nearly the whole way to the recycling bins. I separated the trash into the appropriate receptacles. Mom was close behind.

"It was nice meeting you, Imani and Brena," he said. He smiled thinly.

"Mmhm," I said. I wrapped my arm in Mom's and leaned my head on her shoulder.

"It was nice meeting you, Teddy," Mom said. "By the way, what's your dog's name?" Mom! I tugged her arm.

"Oh." His smile widened as he looked down at his familiar. The dog smiled back. "Her name is Adu!"

"Odaba, Teddy and Adu." She waved. "Let's go home sweet girl," Mom whispered to me as she gently stroked my braids.

3

Tuesday

"Mom! Do you know where all my notebooks are?" I redistributed and relocated as many boxes as I could to avoid unpacking while I looked for my stories. Writing had become my soothing method again. I made a quick promise to myself to get the contents out of the boxes and put them where they belonged by the end of the week to alleviate my guilt. I knew it was a loose promise.

The apartment was unlike anything we'd had in Chicago. The size alone separated it from our south side home. It sprawled the length of at least three of our old apartment. My bedroom was down the hall from Mom's, separated by a bathroom and a very long hallway. I had all the privacy I needed.

The decor made it especially unique. Each room was shrouded in high, vaulted ceilings with red and black checkered squares. The floors had black hardwood throughout. The crown molding and baseboards matched the red in the ceilings, a kind of vermillion. Brass light fixtures and brass-framed mirrors were placed on the walls throughout the home.

I found myself being able to find the positive in situations again. Luckily, the size of our new home and the eggshell-colored walls were things I could count as beneficial. The walls brought brightness into an otherwise grim setting. I also appreciated the creativity. It was clear from the exterior that the apartment building used to be a very large home that had been renovated into apartments. I tried to envision what purpose the rooms in our apartment used to serve in the mansion. The expansive built-in bookcases in the living room indicated that some part of the apartment probably used to be an office.

I traveled down the long hallway from my bedroom, past several mirrors and antique-looking light fixtures, past the bathroom with the walk-in shower and clawfoot tub, and into Mom's room.

"Mom...have you seen the box with my notebooks?" I stopped at the doorway. "Mom?" I gasped.

Sweat slid from Mom's coiled loc updo down her face. She lay in bed with her eyes closed, her chest heaving in labored motions. I rushed to grab a washcloth from her bathroom, ran cold water on it, and returned to place it on her feverish forehead. Her eyes cracked slightly open as the bed shifted with my weight.

"Imani?"

"Mom?"

"I don't feel well."

We both let out a small chuckle at Mom's statement of the obvious. I wiped the sweat from her face before placing the washcloth on the nightstand. "I'm gonna get you some water. I'll be right back," I said, already halfway out of the room.

I caught my reflection in the antique mirror on the hallway wall just before the kitchen entrance. Worry furrowed in the crease of my eyebrows. I moved to the kitchen and got a glass of water from the sink. Water spilled over the lip of the glass and onto my hand. Without wiping it up, I headed back towards Mom's room, catching another glance of myself in the mirror. I ignored the weird notion tugging at me that my reflection stood empty-handed and turned to watch me walk down the long hallway.

"Here, Mom. Sit up." I lifted her head and gently put the glass of water to her lips. She sipped slowly for a few seconds before motioning me to put the glass down.

"Thank you, baby. I'm okay. Just let me rest." She closed her eyes and released a soft snore within moments.

"I'll make you some soup for when you wake," I said out loud, shrugging to myself weakly. Just a few days in a whole new place and Mom was already sick. She'd always taken care of me and now, with her sick— *Well, not always*, I thought, pushing down the painful memory she never wanted me to talk to her about. My stomach dropped. I tried to ignore all the nagging questions I had for her, adding to the list why we never talked about *it* on top of why she never told me we were from Tiwa.

I stopped at the mirror near the kitchen again and examined myself from head to toe. Dressed in a large t-shirt and loose-fitting athletic pants, I couldn't see much of my curvy figure. The sports bra and the pants were doing the job I intended. I peered into the eyes of my reflection, looking for the old Imani. The Imani that hadn't been...

I set aside the thoughts again, made my way to the kitchen, and focused on the recipe I would use for the soup. Mom had taught me so many different soups for different ailments. I wasn't sure what was going on with her now, but maybe some pepper soup with chicken she'd taught me would help speed up her recovery.

I chopped onions with intention, imagining the ingredients coming together as a whole to cure Mom of the mysterious ailment. I needed her to get better soon. I was starting at the community college tomorrow and she was supposed to start her job as one of the Horticulturists for Ibeji Village. Plus, I just really needed her in this new place. She was my guide. I prepared the soup, believing...*knowing* the healing the soup would give her, just the way she had taught me.

"The intention is the most important part," Mom had said, stirring a pot of pepper soup. "Along with the seasoning," she added. We both laughed while she showed ten-year-old me the best way to prepare the pepper soup. We were making it for an elderly neighbor who had been bedridden for days. I remembered the sprightly neighbor bringing back the empty container and her gratitude the following day.

I smiled at the memory and continued working on the soup. "She'll be okay," I told myself, ignoring my own doubts.

4

Wednesday

Fall's fingers barely grazed the Tiwa sky. A crisp breeze wound through the trees before hugging my bare arms. I clutched myself while trying to diagnose the hollow feeling in my stomach. Had to be first day jitters for college. I giggled to myself, remembering how it had felt to wake up and prepare for my first day at Blomberg Preparatory High School in Chicago. The anxiety of being a freshman, fitting in, and wearing the right clothes. When *he* became my first friend. Ugh. The hollow feeling scooted to the unseen depths of my belly. I immediately worked to ground myself by listing something from each of my five senses. Just as I was taught to do.

I paused on the sidewalk where most people were entering Ibeji Village Community College. The sprawling campus held multi-storied buildings within view. Most of the buildings in Tiwa had stone statues guarding the entrances. The college was no different. The windows on the campus had mirrored glass, reflecting either the sky, the multi-colored leaves on the trees, or the stone the building had been made from. The design of the campus surprised me almost as much as our new apartment did. Like the apartment, the campus wasn't like anything I'd seen in Chicago, but it also wasn't very different. I reminded myself that

Tiwa still sat on the same land as the United States and there would be some similarities. The differences were intriguing though.

On the outskirts of the campus, domesticated animals lounged. Students gave them commands and the animals followed the directives, staying in one place or finding another in the shade or closer to other animals. "Familiars," I said aloud to no one. I'd read about how animals were used for companionship, protection, and various Magic spells in Tiwa. When a child reached puberty, they have the choice of choosing an animal familiar: an animal that they are able to link and share consciousness with. Through a series of meditations- taught to the child by their parents and other community leaders- they identify which animals they can link with. Then, when they are ready- as determined by them and their community- they choose the animal they want to link with. The animal lives a normal life span. Once it dies, the person can choose another one, either from the same or different species. When the person is linked with the animal, they can see what it sees and vice versa.

Did I miss my chance to have a familiar? I added that to my mental list of things to ask Mom if she decided to open up.

The group of young women passing me on their way into the college had an accent that was a mixture of a southern drawl with West African tonation. Their clothing, all different in style, still contained the bright, vibrant colors traditional to Ibeji Village. Purples, yellows, and reds, like at the festival. I liked how these outfits were still casual but honored the I.V. Was I already picking up the lingo?

I slipped a small piece of candy into my mouth, one I carried just for these moments, and let the peppermint flavor melt on my tongue. I'd have to go shopping later. My extra-large black shirt and matching sweatpants were not going to cut it here. I fingered the orange, furry, plush ball attached to my shoulder bag. At least I had something bright on me. A familiar scented cologne wafted towards me as I neared the buildings.

I wriggled my nose when I saw Teddy from a distance ambling down the concrete path, heading straight toward me. It was him smelling and looking like a tall, cold glass of lemonade on a hot humid day. Good.

"Hey, stranger. Ba wo ni?" Teddy called out.

"Hi," I replied, looking straight ahead. "I mean, Ba wo." There was no escaping him now.

"If I would have known you were coming to the college, I would have offered to show you around."

Rude did not seem to work with this one, so I tried walking slowly away from him. "Thanks, no tour needed. Where's your beast?" I shook my head. "Never mind. Can you just tell me where this building is?" I asked, pointing to the schedule listed on my phone. "I don't want to be late on my first day."

He took the phone from my hand, grazing my fingers. I moved back a little. I looked up at him as he read the class schedule. The dark thick eyebrows above his hazel eyes furrowed as he tried to locate where my finger had been pointing. I took another look at his muscular body.

Don't do it, Imani, I warned myself, but couldn't stop myself. The flirt was about to exit. "You play ball?" I asked, distracting him from the task at hand. *Noooo, Imani, you did it.*

Teddy's thick lips opened into a wide grin, letting his perfect teeth become the center of attention on his well sculpted face. He handed my phone back to me. I blushed at the smile, and then quickly fixed my face.

"Yes, I play ball. Well, I play a lot of different sports," Teddy answered coolly. "And my beast, or Adu, is at home. We don't go everywhere together. So, your first class is Dr. Pike's History of Tiwa class."

"Mmhm."

"Well, that's my first class, too. It's a requirement for all freshmen. Looks like we're in the same section." His tone became even and matter-of-factly. "You want to walk with me there?"

I regained my senses and was able to look through Teddy again, instead of at him. This was the easiest way to take him in. "Sure."

"How has the move been? How long has it been since you've been back in Tiwa?" Teddy asked, his eyes narrowed with curiosity.

He was acknowledging what was already common knowledge. Only people born in Tiwa could get into Tiwa. They could move to the mainland of the United States and back to Tiwa. But those born on the mainland were rejected by the magic of Tiwa from entering. I wanted to tell him I never dreamed I'd be seeing Tiwa outside of books. That I had believed my entire life that I was born on the mainland. That I just found out recently, I was Tiwan. I wanted to talk, especially since Mom had gotten sick so quickly after arriving in Tiwa. He was nice enough. I gave myself permission to let go for a moment, anyway.

"It was nice, at first, seeing Tiwa after only reading about it in books." I looked up at him. "I didn't know we were from Tiwa. My mom never told me."

Teddy's eyes widened. "What?! Why didn't she tell you?"

I winced. "I don't know. We haven't been able to talk about it. She's sick right now."

Teddy looked down at me with a raised eyebrow. I squished the orange ball on my bag and looked ahead.

"I'm sorry to hear that," he said.

"Thanks. Almost as soon as we got moved into the apartment, she started not feeling well. The Helpers got the furniture in there and we were about to start unpacking boxes when she needed to lie down. She's just been in bed most of the time since then and I've been trying to make sure she eats and drinks enough liquid."

"Oh. Did you try the Helper's Clinic? Where do you live? I can tell you where one is near you."

My body stiffened momentarily then relaxed. I knew I needed to help Mom. I didn't know much about Tiwa, let alone Ibeji Village. But I also did not know enough about this man. I let go again, careful to give him only the information he needed to know. "We live in Yardley Place. Do you know where that is?" I replied. I wondered if he could hear the strain in my voice.

"Oh." Teddy was silent. For longer than a moment. I usually relished moments where people weren't stifling the hush with unnecessary words. This, however, started to get uncomfortable. I clenched the plush in the palm of my hand.

"Ba wo ni, Teddy?" a young woman's voice called out with a lilt. We paused and turned to see a woman about our age walking down the pathway. I took in her whole vibe. She wore a lilac-colored, pleated tennis skirt with a white button-up shirt. Cowrie shells adorned her shoulder-length, curly, natural hair and she wore a multi-colored necklace and matching bracelet. Nothing out of place. Everything was attractive. I knew this type of girl.

"Ba wo ni? And you are?" the woman said, stopping in front of me, slowly scanning me from head to toe, her face contorted with disdain.

"Loreen," Teddy interrupted, "this is Imani. She just moved here from-"

"Oh, are you from Ofo? Hm." Loreen chipped in.

"I'm from Chicago," I straightened up and replied. From the lady's tone, it sounded like Ofo was an insult. I made a note to look at a map and figure it out later. The orange fluff on my bag was close to being pulled off.

"Chi-cah-go?" Loreen repeated slowly. "But you're here in Tiwa. So where are you from in Tiwa?" Loreen's body language demanded an answer.

I stared through her and frowned.

Teddy stepped between us and ushered Loreen away from me. "I'm sure you two will find you have a lot in common. Loreen, we're headed to Dr. Pike's class. What's your first class?"

Loreen swung her hair from her shoulder. The cowrie shells clicked in response. The smell of lavender graced my nose. "Well," Loreen began. "It just so happens, I also have Dr. Pike's class." Loreen looked over and met my eyes. "I'm sure we'll have sooo much in common," she sneered as she headed towards an open door in the building in front of us.

"That's us," Teddy informed Imani, pointing to where Loreen was headed.

"Of course, it is," I replied.

5

"We are the descendants of the formerly enslaved. We are all brothers and sisters, no matter if we are on the mainland or here in Tiwa," Dr. Pike began her lesson. Her footsteps echoed as she paced the rows of the classroom's stadium-style steps, carrying a tablet. A shawl of sunshine spread through the windows, gently touching the locs, twists, and other afro textured hairstyles in the classroom. The hairstyles here were so very similar to the ones back home. I mean, home in Chicago.

"However, the magic of Tiwa is only within the direct descendants of the Rebellion of 1842, when the enslaved from several counties of what was known as North Carolina banded together under the leadership of the Yoruba priestess, Ijapeluidan-" Dr. Pike continued.

"Ija!" a chorus rang out from the class. I jumped in my seat a bit.

"To harness the power within themselves, nature, and the Orisha to free themselves and claim North Carolina as ours. As Tiwa," Dr. Pike said, without missing a beat. "In this course, we'll start with the aftermath of the Rebellion. The building of Tiwa, the protections put into place-"

"I learned this as a child, Dr. Pike." I turned around to the sound of a voice coming from a young woman with ornately braided hair covered in tiny silver rings. She had purple ribbons woven throughout the braids and the most disinterested look I had ever seen in a classroom. And that was saying a lot. The young woman started again. "Why are we learning this repeatedly?" Groans of agreement rang out in the class.

"Well, Ms...?" Dr. Pike looked at the girl and referred to her tablet.

That must've been where she kept the list of students enrolled in the class. "What is your name?" She adjusted the spectacles that slid to the end of her bell pepper-shaped nose. One of her locs slipped out from the high bun on her head.

"Yvette," the young lady replied. "And I apologize for interrupting you," she added with a slight bow to her head. Dr. Pike took her time walking to the front of the classroom, letting the class stew in the tension.

"Yes, well, Yvette," she finally said, placing the tablet down on the lectern in front of her and tucking the stray strand back in place, "it is important that we reiterate the history of Tiwa for numerous reasons. One is that the safety of Tiwa depends on the prayers of the Helpers at the entrance. And the prayers of the Helpers-"

"Depend on our belief, faith, and continued use of prayer and meditation ourselves," Yvette interrupted again. My face grimaced. Even I knew better than to keep interrupting the professor.

Dr. Pike pushed her glasses to the end of her nose and looked over them at the young lady. Yvette squirmed in her seat before looking down at her desk.

"Yes...Yvette. As well as our magic. And, two, this class is not only about the history of Tiwa. It is also important to learn about the history of Ibeji Village. Whether you are from the Land of Awujo, Ibeji Village, or Village of Iku- where I am from- understanding the history of where you come from will help you understand who you are." Dr. Pike walked from behind the lectern and sat on the table adjacent to it. "And, third, not everyone knows the history of Tiwa..."

I could feel someone's burning gaze on the side of my face. I looked over to meet Loreen's stare. Why did this girl have to sit next to me? I glanced at Teddy sitting on the other side of her. He was focused intently on Dr. Pike. Loreen sneered at me then slowly turned to face the professor. What a -.

"As not everyone has had *my* history class and been able to experience all the knowledge I have as a member of the Cult of Emi. The Helper Historians." Dr. Pike giggled at her self-aggrandizing joke. She did a few taps on her tablet and a screen came down behind her, the projector in front of her turned on, and the room's lights turned off. It was fancy fancy in here. "But since you all know so much about Tiwa, let's begin with Ibeji Village today and some important people."

All the names of towns and villages being thrown about swirled around in my head like a whirlwind. I remembered driving through some of the places on our journey to the coast, where Ibeji Village stood. But they had all blended together, even as Mom tried to explain the different traditions honored in each place. The Prayer Helpers at the entrance to Tiwa were the most memorable part of the trip.

"Another founding family, the Yardleys, were a longstanding part of Ibeji Village's counsel of Helpers that ended with Raymond and Elizabeth Yardley," Dr. Pike droned on in the background of my attention.

I was trying to listen but couldn't help thinking about the Change of the Prayer Helpers. It was by chance we got to witness the Change while we had waited to be let into Tiwa. Our timing in our arrival was just right. I was grateful for that.

"They dedicate their lives to the protection of the Tiwa," Mom had said. "In return, like everyone in Tiwa who gives back to the community, they are blessed with shelter, food, water, clothing, education-really, all they need to survive and thrive."

I'd thought about that. "What do you mean everyone in Tiwa who gives back to their community? What happens if you don't give back?" What did I have to give to a place I didn't even know I was a part of?

Mom smiled. She didn't get what I was asking. "What I should have said was that everyone gives back to the community in Tiwa. We all have a role to play. How we give is based on our individual passions, talents, abilities, and desires. We are all taken care of in Tiwa. This'll be very different from Chicago."

She had said that last part like I didn't know. I remembered fear and awe filling my body like a mixture of oil and water in a bottle. I was up to the challenge of learning more about my new home but what did that mean for what I was already dealing with? What did being on the outer land so long mean to how I'd be received here? Did I know enough to even start to understand what it meant to be Tiwan? Everything was so different. The books I read had not fully captured anything I'd seen up until now.

I remembered watching the Prayer Helpers leave single file in single rows, with a different colored row following immediately behind to replace them and continue the prayer. Each row was dressed in the same color but the rows were all different colors from the others, making a moving rainbow of murmured Prayer Helpers. "It's beautiful," I'd whispered.

"...how you set up your altar is up to you and a more involved and detailed discussion in the Altars and Shrines course." Dr. Pike interrupted my inner thoughts, reminding me of the altar Mom always had set up in her room. The pictures of people I'd never met on the altar should have been a sign for me long ago. A hollow feeling in my stomach grew deeper into emptiness. *Why didn't you tell me we were from Tiwa,* I thought to myself. *Why didn't you ask her on the way here,* I replied back. A poke to my right side brought my attention back to class.

I turned sharply and saw Loreen pulling her arm away after poking me. This girl had nerve. She needed to keep her hands to herself. She was lucky my friend, Keisha, wasn't here. Keisha wasn't as calm as I was in these situations. Loreen may have found herself hurt. Unaware of my thoughts threatening bodily harm, Loreen scowled and pointed her finger at Dr. Pike, who was concluding the class.

I rolled my eyes, gathered up my notebooks and gave Loreen enough time to get out the door before I headed outside myself. I gave myself enough time for my anger to pass. I covered my eyes to adjust to the blinding sun after leaving the dark classroom. Upon regaining my sight, I saw Teddy talking to Loreen and excusing himself to walk over to me. Loreen's frown was inescapable. Oh well.

"Hey, mainlander, how was your first class in Tiwa?" Teddy asked. His grin was wide and enticing.

"Interesting," I said. I had one foot turned and ready to walk off. I'd hoped that my body language would hint towards a brief conversation. "A lot more information than the books I've read about Tiwa," I said.

"Books cannot do it justice. Especially to a mainlander. How about a tour of the I.V. from the I.V.'s finest?" Teddy's grin tightened into a tiny smile. Was he nervous?

"Who's that? Do I get to meet someone new?" I joked, looking around Teddy as if someone else was going to walk up.

Pain quickly flashed across his face just as quickly as insight filled it back up. "Oh, you're joking. Ha. What do you say? Can I give you a tour of Ibeji Village?"

I looked past Teddy, at a waiting Loreen. She'd watched peripherally, pretending to not be interested in our conversation. "Hey, Loreen?" I called out. Her head bobbed up in anticipation.

"Yes?" she asked as if perturbed to be disturbed.

"Will you also be joining Teddy to show me around on this grand tour of Ibeji Village? It's the only way I'll go."

Both Teddy and Loreen's eyes widened with curiosity, although Teddy's was more akin to shock. He'd probably never had a woman ask another woman to join them. Especially not Loreen.

"Okay. When?" Loreen asked. She was up to the challenge. I knew she would be. I was relieved. I wasn't sure that I was ready to be alone with a boy again. Not yet. As long as Loreen kept her hands off me, we'd be good.

I turned back to Teddy. "My mom is sick. You said you would tell me where the Helper clinic is near me. You seemed familiar with Yardley Place."

"Yea, of course," Teddy said and pulled out his phone. "What's your phone number? I'll text it to you."

I gave him my phone number, under Loreen's watchful gaze. She had moved closer to us. "You should take it, too, Loreen. Just in case this guy stands me up," I said with an honest smile.

"Take mine," Loreen huffed. She, once again, threw her hair over her shoulder in an overexaggerated act of annoyance.

After all the information was exchanged, I shared that I had to make sure my mom was okay before going on the tour. "Maybe after class tomorrow? If my mom is feeling better," I said, looking into Teddy's hazel eyes. Just off his looks alone, I understood why Loreen hovered around him.

"Yep." Teddy stared back. I wondered what was behind that stare. And if Loreen was ever a recipient of it. Mmm.

"Yea, okay," Loreen interrupted. "Teddy, are you still going to walk me to my next class?"

"I have to go to my next one anyway. Creative writing," I said.

"You write?" Teddy said, raising one eyebrow. "What do you write?"

"Let's go, Theodore," Loreen said, pulling his arm.

"Bye, you two." I waved at them, smiling. *This should be interesting*, I thought to myself as I looked up my next class on my phone. "Now where the hell is this building at?" I said aloud to no one. A bird, flying directly above my head, whistled in response.

Yup, interesting.

6

"Mom! I'm home!" The sound of my voice reverberating through the apartment was the only reply I received. I didn't know if I'd get used to how sound carried in our new home. I tossed my backpack on the sofa in the living room and headed down the hallway to Mom's room. A shiver ran down my spine when I laid eyes on her.

When we had moved in, I was initially offended but eventually impressed with how quickly the Moving Helpers brought the furniture in and set it all up. At first, it felt like they didn't even want to be in the apartment. I was worried everything would be thrown in haphazardly. Once they were done, though, I could tell they were just efficient. Without Mom's direction, they'd set up her queen size bed and its large headboard in the center of her longest wall, away from the door. Matching the rest of the apartment, her room had the red and black checkered ceiling, red molding, black hardwood floors, and was much larger than the one she'd had in Chicago. The solid wood twelve drawer dresser, its attached mirror, a nightstand, and the bed as a part of the matching set still did not fill the room up. The room felt uncomfortable and cold. She'd promised she'd get the decor up and maybe add a desk to the room once we got more settled in. Of course, her altar was set up, but now it sat unattended with an already forming small layer of dust on picture frames and other items.

The drawn curtains limited the afternoon sun in the room. Shadows reimagined the large bed into a gaping mouth, its red pillowcases and sheets enclosing her small and motionless body in the middle. At first glance, Mom seemed to be willingly swallowed up by the bed. She sat straight against the headboard, staring blankly, panting- her chest rising and falling in quick successions. The light from the two brass fixtures above the headboard drew more shadows around her quiescent body, enveloping her in the darkness. I hurried to her side.

This morning's uneaten breakfast and three full glasses of water sat untouched on the nightstand next to the bed. "You didn't eat or drink anything all day, Mom?" I bent over and replaced a twist of hair that had gotten free from her loc bun. I analyzed everything I could about her current state. Her breath released in uneven waves of desert dryness against my cheek. The warmth and comfort that usually filled her dark brown eyes had been replaced with an icy absence of awareness.

"Mom?"

Her head rotated as if it was stuck in a gelatinous substance, so slow time seemed to stand still. Her unfocused eyes seemed to see something outside of my realm of awareness. My heart pounded in my chest. My mind went blank as I tried to think of anything that could be causing this. I gulped. Once her head finally fully turned to meet my look, her eyes returned their focus. I flinched.

"Hey, baby. How was school?" She spoke normally, then smacked and licked her lips. "Will you bring me a glass of water?"

It took me a moment to understand the question. She repeated it.

"Uh, yea. Here let me help you," I said as I grabbed one of the glasses of water with two shaky hands. Not even the two-hand hold could stop the water from spilling over the top. I couldn't stop shaking. I brought it to her mouth, carefully. Awkwardly. Relieved I didn't sprinkle any water on her. "Um, are you hungry? I can make you something to eat."

Mom sipped the water and swatted the glass out of my hands. Her lips pulled back, baring her teeth. She leaned forward and pushed me away from her. Unable to catch myself, I stumbled onto the floor.

"What the hell are you trying to do, Imani? Poison me. What was in that water?"

I stood and backed up towards the door. When did she get so strong? Why did she put her hands on me? She'd never done that before.

"Stupid, stupid girl," she said and leaned back against the wooden headrest. "You never want to listen. Walking around here like you know everything. The world is going to teach you something, Ee-MAH-nee," she fumed, pronouncing my name with an offbeat staccato. "You didn't listen to me but the world will show you."

Words failed me. Again. I glanced around the room. She'd never spoken to me like this. Not even in heated arguments. Did we ever have heated arguments?

She grew more relaxed in the bed. Her sheets now appeared neatly placed around her as if she'd been tucked in gently. She made direct eye contact with me. "You think you're so strong, Imani. So clever. But you can't even bring me a clean glass of water. I wish you would just go." Her voice was strong and harsh, incompatible with the tranquility of her body.

After a moment, her eyes returned to their normal softness. She swept a shaky hand across her forehead, clearing beads of sweat. Like a light switch, she was back. Nothing but warmth in her large brown eyes. "Could you?" she asked. I stood there.

"Wh- what?" I took another step back to the door, slightly shaking my head.

My racing heartbeat started to slow.

"Could you make me something to eat? Breakfast tasted funny this morning. I didn't feel like getting up to make anything different."

I looked up at the ceiling and blinked away the dampness forming in my eyes. I avoided looking at her, confirmed out loud that I'd fix a plate, and left the room.

On the way to the kitchen, I took a detour to the bathroom. The light switch didn't work when I flicked it up. The afternoon sun shed enough light through the window above the bathtub that I could see myself clearly in the mirror. I leaned down, splashed my face with water, and looked deeply into my own eyes.

Mom's words burned in my head as I stroked and twiddled with my braids. What was going on with her? Was it stress from being sick? From the move? From what happened to me? I couldn't remember a time when Mom had ever really been sick. Whenever she got a sniffle or any other symptom of a pending illness, she'd recover in no time after using her own homemade remedies with herbs from the kitchen garden.

I turned off the water and released a long exhale, easing the heaviness in my chest. I flicked down the light switch that had turned nothing on and went to fix her something to eat.

As I gathered the ingredients from the refrigerator, I recalled the last time Mom and I cooked together, just before the move. "I'm glad we have this opportunity," she'd told me.

"To cook together? We always cook together." I had been peeling carrots.

"To leave Chicago. To go to Tiwa." Mom's focus remained on the pot she was stirring. She lifted the spoon, took a taste, nodded, then replaced the lid on the pot.

"How long has it been since you've been to Tiwa?" I asked, moving on to chopping herbs.

She only smiled at me. "You know what? Let's throw that in there now and leave a little for the garnish. That's just what it's missing." I could tell she was avoiding my question.

I sat in the confusion I'd continued to feel since that night. It covered me like Mom's hugs as I reheated the pepper soup and put it on a tray. The confusion lingered when I returned and found her sitting abnormally straight in her bed, staring blankly. Again.

Mom's refusal of the food she had just asked for came in the way of her not acknowledging me at all. She sat as if she was paralyzed. I placed the plate next to the rest of the day's unfinished food. My pleas to get her out of the room and into some fresh air outside were also ignored.

"What if I open this window, Mom? Let the fresh air come to you?" The setting sun cast shadows through the half-opened curtains on Mom's serene face, adding to the illusion the bed was swallowing her again. Her expression remained vacantly focused on the walls. She remained silent in response to my questioning.

I opened the window anyway. A small breeze gently pushed the black curtains into the room. A voice carried on the wind, its words unintelligible. I went to the window and searched for the source. The street was bare. Most of the stores had closed and had their night lighting on. Homes had begun to turn on their porch lights. Streetlights were lit. I turned to face Mom, plotting how I'd get her to the Helper Clinic. Her legs were on the side of the bed as if she were preparing to stand. She looked through me. The expression on her face was hollow, like a Halloween jack-o-lantern cut into the image of a black woman.

The bed heaved as I sat next to her. I laid my head on her shoulder, closed my eyes, and inhaled the scent that had for so long been a smell of comfort. Memories of the times when she would hold me close at church returned. Her perfume would envelop me as she clapped and sang along with the gospel music. Or, when the church would pray for me after "the tragedy," it was Mom's scent that helped me feel safe. Now, it served as a reminder that something was not okay.

A groan brought me back to the present. I lifted my head and opened my eyes to find Mom's eyes wide, staring at me intensely. The strange voice sounded again. Stronger this time. It accompanied a rush of wind that tossed the curtains into the room. A chill crawled at a snail-like pace down my back.

"M-mommy?"

She didn't break her look. I was trapped in her gaze, unable to move. My heart thumped loudly. I could see her face but was not seeing her. It wasn't Mom that I was looking at. Her eyes glowered as they had done earlier when she verbally attacked me. The voice from the window became louder, clearer. "You have returned and I have you again." Mom mouthed the words, but the sound was carried on the wind from the window. She reached out and grabbed my wrist, her mouth continuing to form the words from the wind. "You have returned and I have you now."

"You're hurting me, Mom," I whispered. I writhed, tears falling, as the sharp pain got worse. "Please," I cried. Her fingernails scratched my skin as I snatched my arm out of her grip. I stood up and away from the bed. "Mom, stop!" The pull of my arm had pushed her into a lying position, her feet dangling over the side of the bed. The curtains stood soldier-still as the wind abruptly stopped.

Mom had stopped her silent mouthing. She blinked and actually looked at me. She was back. I could see my mother in there again. She straightened out her legs and stretched back into the bed. The blanket was tugged out of its tucked corners as she pulled it over her and rolled away from me.

"It's cold, baby. Close the window." I backed away from her to close the window. I heard her begin to snore softly. I kept my eye on her as I left the room and went back into the bathroom.

The light switch didn't work again. I barely noticed. The glow from the streetlights below the window wasn't strong but there was enough light. I leaned on the countertop and studied my reflection in a slight daze. What was going on? What had I just witnessed? The eyes in the mirror suddenly blinked while mine were open. I froze. Was this my imagination? The reflection of the illumination from one of the streetlights flickered before it went out. Slivers of light from the hallway was all I had now. A cold awareness that something strange was going to happen again lingered in my chest.

I remained focused on my mirrored image. It smiled unpleasantly. I closed my eyes and shook my head. The image continued to sneer at me when I looked back. It rolled up vertebrae by vertebrae until it had fully straightened its body. The noncompliant reflection cocked its head from side to side, its grin widening and growing more sinister. *Run!* I thought at my feet. The mirror's image bent its arms slowly in a stacco motion until its long skinny hands were on its hips. *RUN.*

My feet padded down the long hallway, sweeping me out of the bathroom and into my bedroom. The sound of my door slamming and the lock engaging echoed through the apartment. I stayed awake as long as I could, waiting for the scary version of me to wiggle the doorknob.

7

Thursday

I needed an escape. I'd dozed off and on throughout the night, waking up late and missing my classes. I was surprised I even got any sleep after last night. I decided to straighten up around the apartment and take the trash out. Getting out of the apartment would be a good break from yesterday's weirdness.

I peeped in on Mom from her doorway. She appeared to be sleeping under the covers. I didn't take too long to be sure. I figured leaving for a few minutes would be okay. *New place, new home, new shit,* I thought to myself, grabbing the cloth bag of garbage.

"Mom, I'm taking out the trash!" I called out from the front door. The sound of the door banging against the door jamb was loud enough to shroud any response she may have made. But I knew she didn't say anything.

The canvas bag, full of recyclables and compostables, made me lean a bit to the side as I made my way down the basement. The memory of Mom teaching me to sort through the garbage popped in my head. Paper, glass, cardboard, and organic compost materials. I realized that there'd been no official recycling program where we had lived in Chicago, but Mom had still been adamant about it. I was starting to notice that a lot of her habits and behaviors had roots in Tiwa. How could I miss something so obvious?

At least I'd be able to take my time sorting everything and be away from that apartment. I headed for the stairs that led from the second floor to the first-floor lobby. My feet made little noise on the black tile that covered the floors outside the apartment. The silence of the building was loud. Stifling. The glass in the bag banged around, reverberating throughout the building. I realized it was the only sound I heard from the place. I noted that I had not seen any neighbors yet or heard any kids. "This place is so creepy," I said aloud. At least there was comfort in hearing my own voice.

The lobby of the building was expansive. I could see how great the foyer of the mansion had once been. An extravagant brass chandelier seemed to be part of the original decor that the renovators decided to keep. It wasn't as modern as some of the other light fixtures in the place. The front door was large and wooden with electronic security features. I imagined, based on the size, that the one door was previously two fancy doors that led into the mansion. I smiled at my own creative revisioning of the mansion as it had once been and headed to explore the first floor.

Past the lobby, I carefully examined the apartment doors on the lower floor, starting with the right side of the building. I knew one of the doors should open to the stairs that led to the basement. It was common for apartments in Tiwa to have an interior central place for the recyclables. I'd found that out in my reading.

Each apartment was labeled with iron numbers next to the black wooden doors. Before I reached the left side of the building, I found an unmarked door in the center back of the building. I twisted the knob and found it was unlocked. The door opened to a stairwell made of concrete, with bright overhead lights and a sign on the wall that read "Recycling" with an arrow pointing down. I cheered softly as I headed down the stairs.

The basement was filled with four large, variously colored bins. I glanced around. This was the least decorated part of the building I'd seen so far. Blank cement walls and floors matched the cement stairs. Aside from the bins, the room was empty. It was also cold. I hugged myself and rubbed my arm. This room was quieter than the lobby, if that was even possible.

I could barely smell the normal decomposition that comes with garbage and wondered how often the bins were emptied. Must've been some sort of Tiwan magic I didn't know about yet. Something to keep the smell down.

After figuring out which bin was which, I started tossing garbage into them. The clank of the bottles and the smoosh of the organic materials were soothing. Instead of being efficient and gathering multiple items of the same material to place in their respective bins, I took my time. I removed one individual item out of the large canvas bag and walked to its respective bin. I listened for the thud to signal that the bottle had fallen to the bottom of the huge colored bins. Then I started the process again. Unable to hear the paper or organic garbage, I counted to ten between dumping them. Anything to draw out the time I could spend outside of the apartment.

I threw the last empty jar into the blue bin. I rolled the canvas bag up, tucked it into my arm, and headed towards the stairs. A faint clicking on the basement floor stopped me. I peered further into the basement, looking for a dropped bottle. A floral scent clogged my nostrils. It started off sweet, then became cloying and unbearable. The smell grew stronger and the room started to change. The garbage bins disappeared. In their place, children's toys and books lined the walls which were now painted in pastels and covered with children's drawings. A plush cream-colored carpet expanded from wall to wall. I found myself in a playroom.

A smiling woman dressed in a long yellow dress and long braids scurried out of the cellar rooms and down the hallway, chasing a giggling little girl. The little girl wore a dress similar to the woman's. Her large puff of billowy afro hair bobbed with her steps. The woman chased after the girl, approaching where I stood at the bottom of the stairs. A sense of familiarity washed over me as I watched the two get closer. I sucked in my breath. The little girl looked just like...me.

I spun around towards the basement stairs, trying to avoid a collision between me, the woman and the girl. Instead of the cement stairwell that led straight up to the lobby, I narrowed my eyes at a set of stairs made of black hardwood and a shiny black handrail spiraling up towards a heavy wooden door with articulate woodworking design. Several brass light fixtures, similar to the ones I had in my apartment, brightened the stairway and playroom. My heart rate quickened as my thoughts exploded. Where was I? How would I get out of here? Who was the little girl quickly approaching me, as if she was running into my arms? I tripped over my feet and stumbled on the bottom step. Inches away from me, the little girl and the woman vanished, evaporating into the air. I blinked rapidly, watching the bins that held the recyclables return. The cream-colored carpet receded into nothingness as the drab cement floor once again replaced it. My feet and heart matched a quickened pace as I ran back up the concrete stairs and into my apartment.

8

Then

The clanging of utensils and chatter of small talk ceases abruptly when the host rises from the head of the large table, his glass in hand. "Eshe! And welcome! My wife and I," he points his glass to the woman seated next to him, "are so excited that you all could join us for tonight's festivities."

The woman does not shine as bright as her husband. Her clothing is neat and fit, but small frays and tiny stretches give away the time and care she's taken into keeping them as close to new as possible. As if she knew upon receipt of the long purple dress that it would be one of the only pieces she would receive for a long time. A notable contrast to the shiny newness of her husband's suit. The woman lifts her head high enough to catch the eye of her husband, smiles meekly, and returns to looking down at the table.

"I just returned this morning from the mainland," the host continues, "and I couldn't wait to see my friends again." His voice carries across the dining hall, where all of his twenty or so guests are gratuitously spread out. He pauses a moment, allowing the guests an opportunity to force their cheers and imitate their delight at his return. There are no replies from the tables. He sees only the admiration and awe held in their eyes.

It is either complete oblivion or willful ignorance that he fails to see the contempt that plainly shows on their faces.

Most are only present for the gossip, the gaudiness of the host, visual proof of how he treats those "poor girls." A smaller few hope their presence will earn a reward of some kind from the host. None are here for his friendship.

"I've added another subsidiary on the mainland that will contribute to the continued success and growth of Ibeji Village. Business is good!" he laughs. Helpers begin exiting from the kitchen, balancing multiple trays of food and drink. With fluid choreographed motion, they stand behind the guests and place drinks down first, then food from the left. "What you give, you get ten times over. The help is now presenting you with some of the delicious new dishes I was able to try while on the mainland. Eshe, enjoy. We will begin the games after the meal."

The guests silently take in the various colors and textures on their plates. "Another one of his concoctions," one says before slowly chewing the creation, working to maintain a look of pleasure on his face in case the host happens to look in his direction. The guest's wife swallows slowly with a grimace. "I wonder what game he will think of tonight," she whispers, watching tears fall from one of her husband's eyes.

"I can't believe he's managed to make something more disgusting than last time," the husband replies a little too loudly once he's managed to swallow his bite. The host turns his head in the direction of where the comment was made. The husband and wife return to their plates and begin eating voraciously without any additional comment.

The host, unable to decipher the source of criticism, signals to the Helper child standing near the wall. "Boy, bring me the game." The child nods, his fluffy afro shaking along with his head. He runs to the kitchen and returns with a flat wooden box. His arms wriggle to balance its unwieldiness. He hands it to the host. The host snaps in the child's face. The boy pulls a cloth from his apron and simultaneously clears the plates and wipes the host's space. A woman Helper comes from behind, scratches her fingers in his hair, and gently slides him to the side. The boy looks up at her, smiles, hands her the dishes, and moves out of the way. The woman gives a quick squeeze to his shoulder and finishes cleaning the host's space. The boy's fluffy afro wiggles with him as he retreats to his spot on the wall and waits, patiently.

The host waves the woman away once the space is cleared. With great dramatic flair, he slams the box on his table. The glasses and plates of the guests he shares the table with bounce up and down. None of the guests make a sound. He clicks the box open and stands, waiting. The talking dies down and all eyes are on him.

"Who would like to play a game with me?" he sneers, his voice lowered to add to his theatricality.

The little girl that sits next to his wife darts out of her chair. She is big for her age. Her clothing is nearly too small and holds the similar wear and tear of the woman next to her, but she shines nearly as bright as her host. "I want to play, Daddy." She raises her hand. The other guests laugh at the naivete of the child. The host scowls at his daughter and then at the laughing guests.

"This game is not for you," he says through clenched teeth. A forced smile plasters upon his lips. "Why don't you go to your room and read? Your dinner is done." He motions to the child standing on the wall "Boy!" The boy's eyes grow large and he attends to the host, his feet scurrying as fast as they can go.

The boy sneaks a glance at the little girl before meeting the host's angry gaze. "Yes sir?"

The man points his glower at the girl. "Escort the child to her bedroom. Her evening is finished."

"I never get to play," she mutters under her breath, pushing her chair under the table. Her long-braided pigtails swing with fury. The woman lifts her head from her plate and reaches out to her daughter. The child leans in to her mother for a hug and a gentle stroke of her head.

"I'll be in later to help you to bed," the mother whispers. Utters of "Aww" and "that's her baby" fill the room. The girl leaves her mother, ignoring everyone else- including the little boy that waits quietly to escort her to her room.

The boy doesn't seem to mind being ignored. He watches the host's furrowing eyebrows relax into appall and indignation as his daughter turns her nose up at him when she passes. The boy is delighted but keeps his face stoic lest he incur the host's wrath.

The daughter traipses down the hall until she is out of view of her parents and the guests. Out of view from everyone, her brightness dims. Her two pigtails sink lower on her well-worn dress from the weight of her hanging head.

"I never get to play," she mutters. "I didn't want to play anyway."

The little boy picks up his pace to match hers as she ventures ahead of him down the long red hallway. She catches his reflection in one of the large brass mirrors that adorns the walls, stops walking, and turns to face him.

"I don't need YOU," she stabs her finger in the center of his chest, "showing me," she pokes him again, "where I need to go. You are the help. I don't need the help."

He should be hurt. His ego is bruised a little. He looks at the girl, who is nearly his age and size, and embraces the touch of her finger on his chest. He tilts his head and smirks at her. She removes her finger from his body and studies him. "You look stupid," she says. She copies his smirk, turns back around, and saunters down the hall. The boy remains in the hallway, his head tilted, a smirk still stuck on his face. He likes her.

After waiting outside the girl's room for some time to make sure she stays put, he heads back to the dining hall. He returns to find the guests making animal sounds and movements. The host is chanting under his breath, excitement and enjoyment plastered on his face. The boy's mother waves him over to the wall with her. She places him behind her, protecting him from the embarrassment of the guests and the host's magic. The boy pokes his head out from his mother's side. He watches a couple pretend to run like ostriches up and down the dining hall, appearing to be racing each other. Another guest slithers on the floor like a snake, sticking his tongue in and out of his mouth. The boy almost giggles out loud at the woman woofing like a dog at her husband, who pretends to be a scared cat. The husband's spine curves and the boy imagines his hair raising all over his body.

"You're doing wonderful! I will soon pick a winner," the host calls out, his hand maneuvering animal toys floating above the opened wooden box. He laughs heartily, looking to his wife to join in on his pleasure. She feels his gaze, looks up from the table, and manages to force a laugh. He kisses her cheek and returns to chanting and laughing at the guests.

The boy is thankful that the girl was spared from the game and glamour magic. He is grateful that he and his mother are Helpers and would never be allowed to play. He is saddened that the guests feel obligated to attend these dinners and play these games. He wonders what kind of man he would be in this situation. The host or one of the guests?

9

Friday

Normality returned to the Bennett household. Somewhat. "Go to class, baby," Mom insisted. Her cheeks were full and the brown of her face was no longer ashen. "I'll be fine until you come back. I'll warm up some food if I get hungry. Here, give me one of those books off the nightstand. Never mind, I'll get it. I'll be fine, child, just go." She got out of the bed and ushered me out of the room. I acted like I didn't notice her labored breathing and the stale stench of illness from her pores as she hugged me goodbye and I rushed out the door to class. She was getting better, I told myself. Maybe she's not as sick.

Sick? Girl, that's what you think she is? I thought to myself, reminded of the foreign voice on the wind and her trancelike state. *Well, that's what I'm calling it for now-* I thought back. *Until I can make sense of it, she's sick.*

After my Creative Writing class, I found myself on campus wishing that I was able to have a normal day at school. The brightness of the sun irritated me. As well as the crispness in the air and the smell of flowers that generally lingered around Ibeji Village- or at least on the school's campus. *Focus, girl, focus.* I counted the inhales and exhales of my deep breaths until I reached ten. I'd practiced the technique multiple times during class today, but it still wasn't working. My mood had not changed. I was shocked at the relief I felt when I saw Teddy and Loreen standing at the edge of campus.

"Imani!" Teddy waved as if he'd noticed me first. I waved back and jaunted a little towards them.

"Ba wo ni?" I greeted the two, proud of myself for remembering.

"Ba wo," the two said in unison, although Loreen barely parted her lips.

"How's your mom? I didn't see you on campus yesterday," Teddy inquired, standing so close to me he was shading me from the sun. It kind of felt good.

"Better. Thanks for asking."

"Eshe," Loreen corrected me.

"I'm sorry?" I asked, turning my whole body to face her. Loreen had lilac throughout her ensemble again. She wore a white blouse, lilac-colored form-fitting slacks, and her hair in one long ponytail that extended high from the top of her head. She had a tiny spotted gecko pin on her collar. The pin moved its head, taking me in as I took in Loreen. "It's a real gecko," I whispered.

"Yes, it's a real gecko," Loreen replied. "And we say 'Eshe' instead of 'Thank you' in Tiwa." Loreen seemed to take an odd pleasure in educating me. The condescension spilled over her words. She flipped her ponytail as if it were the period on her sentence.

I studied Loreen's body language, watching her move closer to Teddy. It was clear she wanted to be more than friends with him and she thought I was interrupting that process. I decided to overlook her tone and the gecko that seemed to mirror her actions. "Well, Eshe, Loreen. And, Eshe, Teddy," I replied, turning my attention back to him. "Mom insisted I get out the apartment and go to school. She didn't want me to call the Helpers. Said she was improving."

"Sounds like today is the perfect day for the tour then." Teddy smiled down at me.

"Huh?" Loreen and I said in unison. We glanced at each other. I gave her my sweetest smile and she rolled her eyes in return. Whatever.

"Let me show you some of my favorite parts of the I.V.," Teddy implored.

I looked at Loreen, my eyes wide with the hope that she would come too. I wasn't ready to go alone with a boy again. Not even Teddy. "Only if you're coming," I told her.

Loreen sighed heavily, like she'd just gotten off an eighteen-hour shift, before answering. "Fine, I'll come." The gecko appeared to roll its eyes. I grinned. I knew that girl wasn't going to let me go off with Teddy alone.

Teddy was affable to both of us coming. "Cool. First stop, the North Entrance," he said.

***

The train ride was nothing like the ones I'd had on the El in Chicago. High-speed trains ran all through Tiwa and Ibeji Village. I was surprised by the cleanliness, quietness, and ease of service. None of the books I'd read prepared me. I followed Teddy and Loreen up the stairs and onto the platform without paying anything. I stopped for a moment, looking for a turnstile or pay machine, refusing to believe it was free. I let Loreen's stare- while she and Teddy waited for me to board- rush me along. A few minutes after boarding the train, we arrived at the Northern Entrance. We walked down the stairs from the platform and headed towards a small hill below the entrance.

I strolled the knoll, admiring the large statue that appeared to watch over everything from the wall above the Northern Entrance to Ibeji Village. It depicted a man with a bare chest looking out over the town, his hands squarely on his hips which led to the tail of a serpent. The African features were undeniable although the statue was cast in gray stone. This one was similar to the one that stood on the wall to the Western Entrance, the one Mom and I had gone through to enter the town. Both statutes were giants with human heads and upper bodies, but the lower body was of a serpent's tail. They were similar, but different somehow. I couldn't yet grasp what the differences were.

"It's a different twin," Loreen advised, seeing the confusion in my eyes. "The Northern and Southern entrances have the Twins of Nummo watching over. The Western and Eastern entrances have the Nummo Twins watching over. They are similar, but...different. The facial expressions are the main differences." She looked back at the statue. "Some say that changes depending on the mood of the viewer. What do you see?"

I studied the statue. It looked both concerned and confused. I turned to reply but Loreen was already walking away. This was probably typical of her behavior. I shrugged it off. I let the weight of what I didn't know about Ibeji Village, or Tiwa for that matter, also lift from my shoulders. *It's out of my control. Be open to learning,* I reminded myself. The vague remembrance of the story of the twin spirits I'd read in one of the books in preparation for the move came to me. "Twins in spirit, twins in the physical. Four altogether," I said aloud.

"Looks like some of your books were helpful," Teddy joked from the comfort of his seat on a rock that faced the entrance. He jumped down and moved closer to me, placing his hand softly on my shoulder. I recoiled, swiped his hand off, and moved a couple of steps away from him. He looked at me, then Loreen. She shook her head and shrugged, not completely sure of Teddy's misdeed. I wasn't either myself. "Sorry," Teddy murmured under his breath.

"It's okay." My voice was soft. "I just get jumpy...when I get touched unexpectedly."

"Got it," Teddy replied. Loreen nodded her head.

"Hey, where's your big dog?" I asked, aware of the feeble attempt to change the subject.

"I thought you were scared of her," Teddy teased. "I left her at home. Would you like her to join us? I can call her."

My face squinted in confusion. "You can call her? From here?"

"Yes. That is how our connection works as a familiar," he said. I appreciated that his tone wasn't condescending, like he didn't mind educating me about Tiwan practices. "I can show you."

I considered his offer briefly. "That's ok. Where's your next favorite place?"

"The park!" Loreen answered. *Hm. Interesting,* I thought to myself. Teddy may have been right about the things we had in common.

***

The children of Ibeji Village had the nicest playground I had ever seen. Held inside large interconnected, circular, greenhouse-type structures, I couldn't help but squeal "Bubbles!", bringing laughter from my classmates. The children had so many choices for play. Some were cooling off at a waterpark. Others climbed and swung from playground equipment sitting atop lush green grass.

"The playground equipment is made from recycled materials," Loreen had informed me before walking away again. I saw children and adults contributing to the community garden as volunteers. This was probably the site where Mom would have started work earlier this week. Unless Ibeji Village had other gardens I hadn't learned about yet. Teddy, Loreen and I joined the families sitting and watching the wildlife in the large forest beyond the Northern entrance, outside of the bubbled greenhouse structures.

"It's so...green," I said from my dropped jaw. The laughter of the children filled my ears. It was a nice reprieve from the building. A lightness I hadn't felt in a long time filled my body. "It's so green," I repeated, "and beautiful."

"I have to admit, I can see how different this is for you, having never been here," Teddy observed. "I've never left Tiwa. I've only heard about the stories of the inequities and impoverished conditions that a lot of the descendants had to live in. Maybe you'll have to tell me more about Chicago."

"That's not all it's about. Chicago has culture and community. It's not the way the media tries to portray it," I said with a glare. "Why are you frowning?" I asked Loreen after seeing her and the gecko's expression. Loreen, her familiar's scowls, and Teddy's denunciation of my home managed to break the spell the park had on me.

Loreen returned my glance and grinned. "Nothing," she answered shortly and walked away, standing behind Teddy.

I turned back towards the forest and centered myself. "Can we stay here for a moment?"

We all moved to sit on the grass closer to the boundary. Loreen sat between me and Teddy. I studied the wind moving through the trees. A bird stood out, flying from tree to tree. It was a cardinal, with a vibrant red color and some yellow and orange. I couldn't figure out if I was following the bird or if it was following me.

The trees were far, but tall. I figured that they were large enough to have covered some of the buildings in downtown Chicago. "That is Iya Forest, the boundary which surrounds the Village of Iku," Teddy said. Loreen laid back on the grass and studied the clouds while he gave some background to the forest and the history of the Village of Iku. "Before Tiwa had Prayer Helpers to protect it, each town had to protect itself. The legend is that the trees were grown tall and wide with magic to protect the Village of Iku. I only know about it from Dr. Pike, since she's from there. But I've never been."

It was almost exhausting to think about all the stuff I had to learn about. I chose to focus on what was in front of me instead and quietly observed the forest.

"My mom always made sure I was outside playing," I interrupted the silence among us. "She made it kind of a game where we would try out different parks and rate them. When I got older and could go on my own, I'd take my friends to some of my favorite parks. Playing like little kids. Slide wars and swing contests. We were the most relaxed...most ourselves at the park." I stopped talking. I lowered my head to focus on the grass I twiddled between my fingers. "The park is where I was most free. One of the only places I could let my guard down..." I continued, my voice trailing off. A river of positive memories flowed into a current of negative ones. I counted my inhales and exhales to slow down my heart rate.

I heard Teddy and Loreen shift in their seats as the change in my energy carried over and traveled to them. Loreen heaved deeply, appearing especially sensitive to the heaviness of what I was holding back. Teddy rose and faced us. "Another spot?" he offered along with his hands.

"Yea," I said. I pulled myself up with one of Teddy's hands. Loreen waited until I was up and took both of his hands to rise from the ground. The three of us headed back to the train station.

***

"Welcome, young people. I am Malini," the shopkeeper greeted us.

Malini was short and curvy with an air of cheery mysteriousness. The smell patchouli drifted into my nose whenever she moved. She wore a magenta floral headband around her tiny afro and a tiny snake was partly wrapped around her neck like a living lavalier. I didn't have to wonder if the snake was real. It seemed to greet us just as the shopkeeper did. Its head moved from side to side, taking in me, Loreen, and Teddy individually as Malini did the same. I decided the snake was harmless to me. I relaxed and perused the store.

Chicago had botanicas here and there that Mom and me had frequented. They had nothing on this shop. The energy and magic that I'd felt only subtly to this point of being in Ibeji Village was now deep in my bones. My body tingled as if small currents of electricity were flowing through me like energy pulses of magic. I walked up and down the aisles, examining the divination tools, statutes, crystals, and other tools that supported the magic of Tiwa and its inhabitants, taking it all in.

Malini was happy to answer all of the questions I threw at her. "That is citrine." She pointed to the light orange crystal I held between my fingers. "It's used for healing and removing toxins from the body."

I placed the crystal back gently in its bin and wandered towards the herbs. From the tarot cards to the palm oil, to the various candles, I toured the shop like a child in a toy store living out their wildest dreams. I asked about every item that sparked my curiosity. The same wonder I felt in the park was even more dazzling now.

"How do you learn about all this stuff? I mean how to use it?" I asked the other two.

Teddy grinned. "Our families are our first teachers. When we enter school, magic is still an integral part of our lives. It's what we do. To help ourselves-"

"And the magic of Tiwa," Loreen and Malini finished in unison.

"And now? How can I learn how to use it now?" I followed up.

"From your family. From your ancestors. From within. The power of the universe starts from inside you," Malini replied.

I beamed. Her answer was vague but for the first time since arriving, I understood how the magic was something more than what I had accepted it to be. Magic in Tiwa was not at all how it was thought of on the mainland. Everyone talked about it like it was some storybook character throwing electricity-filled spells with their magical wooden sticks. Not even the books I read had captured it appropriately. I was starting to feel how innate it was for the Tiwans. And myself. This magic was purposeful and inspired connections between families, ancestors, and the community. My heart swelled at the realization that I was truly part of something special. I wanted to be able to tap into it. I avoided the thoughts about Mom keeping our heritage a secret.

I wished we could have been together for my first visit to the shop. Getting these lessons from her when I was a child, the way other Tiwans did, would have been more meaningful. I didn't even get a chance to get them once we arrived. I pushed past the discomfort of the memory of Mom's strange state those past couple of days, as was my usual way to cope. The day was going well and I wanted to take it in without everything that complicated it.

"What's this?" I asked the shopkeeper. I held up a small plant holder that contained small, circular, purple flowers on a vine. I skimmed the warning label on the pot and sniffed at the flowers and was immediately brought back to the event in the apartment building basement. It was the same scent I had smelt just before seeing myself as a child playing with the strange woman.

"That is morning glory," Malini started. "It has lots of uses. Some good, some not so good. In Tiwa, we try to use magic for good to maintain balance and support the Prayer Helpers. Like anywhere though, not everybody wants good all the time."

I paused. I had to rethink some of what I believed about Tiwa. I'd assumed that everyone was benevolent here and that was one of the stark differences between here and the mainland. But people were people no matter where you were. Bad intentions existed everywhere.

It was something I'd explored with my therapist in the past. Learning not to take the actions of others personal because it wasn't always about me. People were individuals and their motivations didn't reflect anything about who I was. It'd been helpful, at the time, to understand that. To not blame myself.

"Did you want to buy anything?" Malini interrupted my processing, highlighting another similarity between Tiwans and mainlanders. *Always about the money*, I thought, my face screwed with extreme distaste.

"Not always," Teddy said. I took a step back, unsure how he knew what I'd thought. "Most of us do not use money like on the mainland," he continued. "But for the shops of goods that aren't for food, water, or clothing...we use currency to support the abundance of Tiwa. It also allows those who choose to go back and forth to the mainland to get what they need there."

I shrugged. It didn't make much sense to me. "I don't have any money, yet. I haven't had a chance to get any from my mom. I can come back to get the morning glory later."

Teddy pulled out his wallet. "I'll get it. Consider it a 'Welcome Home' gift."

I stiffened up. I didn't know what this gift meant. I wasn't sure of his intentions. *Maybe I'm overthinking*, I thought to myself. *Maybe it's just a gift and that's it.*

"That's ok. Thank you, Teddy," I told him. "I'll come back later. Maybe with my mom." Hopefully.

"I'd be happy to help you with any altar work when you do come back," Malini added. Her snake appeared to nod in agreement, its tongue sliding in and out.

***

"The museum is on the way back. We'll just do a quick run-through," Teddy said. The three of us waited for the next train to come as the sun started to set over the platform. I shrugged.

"It's getting late. I've been gone all day," I said after checking my phone. No missed calls or messages. "Mom's expecting me soon."

"Ok, ok. We'll race through. You have to at least get a glimpse," Teddy continued.

Loreen looked at me and shrugged. I raised an eyebrow at Loreen's lack of snootiness and shrugged back in both reply and acceptance of the small change in her behavior.

The entrance to the museum was simple, yet elegant. Large glass doors with gold lettering reading "Ibeji Village History Museum" welcomed us in. "There are more museums in the I.V.," Teddy acknowledged. "This is just my favorite. Some of the art held here is the best in Tiwa, or so I've been told." I nodded gently, trying not to engage a growing feeling of being overwhelmed. Teddy led us past the Contributors from Ibeji Village section. I glanced at the bust of Garrett Morgan, inventor of the three-light traffic system used on the mainland. I tried to look at the other exhibits of Tiwan descendants that had an impact on the mainland, but Teddy was moving too fast and I wanted to keep up.

Once we arrived at the Artists of Ibeji Village display, I understood why Teddy wanted me to see it. The displays of canvas, interpretive art, and sculptures were all too much for me to take in during this visit. It was all stunning and beautiful at first glance. I couldn't wait to bring Mom back to explore the museum with more time. Teddy led us past most of the art to reach the end of the artists' exhibit. With grand hand movements and flailing arms, Teddy presented his favorite piece.

"This is the Headdress of Ibeji," he informed us. The wooden sculpture had detailed figurines that resembled the Nummo Twins on the top portion of the headdress. Below that, where the wearer's face would fit, were tiny, intricate figures performing essential tasks. Loreen and I leaned in and peered closely at the herbalist with stringed flowers between her fingers, the cook stirring a pot over a single-eyed stove, the drummer with hands stopped mid-motion in the beat of the drum, a flutist with her instrument pressed to her lips and her eyes closed during the passion of the music. I pointed at the mother carrying her child lying where the third eye would be on the wearer.

"This is beautiful, Teddy," Loreen commented, with an exaggerated simper. "I can see why it's your favorite. Eshe. I appreciate you sharing it with me."

Teddy scratched his head and smiled sheepishly. "Eshe, Loreen."

I walked around the headdress, studying it. It was so delicate and powerful. I read the description next to it and found that it was worn in tribute to those who had created and maintained Ibeji Village. "Often worn at the Festival of Ibeji Village," I read aloud, "the headdress celebrates the lives and importance of all the Villagers."

I opened my mouth to continue but hesitated. Something beyond the mask caught my eye. Teddy followed my look and saw the Founders of Ibeji Village exhibit right next to the mask. I walked towards the large drawing of the building posted on the wall of the exhibit. Loreen and Teddy simultaneously took large steps and managed to get in front of me just as I reached the drawing.

"The Yardley Place," I read the title. "This is my apartment building. This is where I live," I said, the importance of what I was saying slowly coming to me.

Loreen hooked my left arm through her right arm and guided me back towards the front. "It's getting late. How's your mom doing?"

I thought for a moment. "You're right," I said, shaking my head to retain clarity. I looked at Loreen's arm hooked through mine and smirked. "Look at you getting all comfortable with me."

Loreen frowned, dropped my arm and stormed ahead of us. Teddy and I snickered and followed her out of the museum.

IO

Silence filled the apartment like a big boulder- heavy and stagnant. I sighed. The moon's tiny fingers of light snuck through my drawn curtains, adding nothing to the already well-lit room. I could see a small sliver of the fullness of the moon through the curtains. That would be a good excuse to distract myself from my school reading.

I stood from my desk and raised my arms and hands to the ceiling and held them there until my entire body had reached its final stretch. I switched off the overhead light in my room and pushed the curtains open wider before flopping on the bed. The moon was completely round and absolutely supple. It reminded me of my old room in Chicago. The way the full moon would watch me in my bed while it illuminated the entire room. At least I had one less thing to miss.

Events of the day flashed in my mind. I smiled to myself, thinking of all the beauty and surprises Ibeji Village had to offer. I could still see the vibrant green from the park and allowed myself to imagine what it would have been like to grow up here. Visiting that park as a child with Mom. And later with friends. My heart dropped in my stomach when I remembered some of the memories I had at the park back home.

I remembered middle school when Keisha and I would be the two running across wooden bridges, climbing up spiraling poles, and gliding down slides. One chasing after the other. Giggles and friendly taunts filling up the park. I shook the memory out of my head when I got to the part of Keisha moving to California during our freshman year in high school. I also shook away the familiar feelings of loneliness, longing, and hurt.

The bed groaned from my weight. The pillow held my head firmly. I traced the moonlight's rays with my finger in the air. A happy memory of Keisha's replacement crossed my mind. I allowed myself to remember. Even as sophomores, he and I had enjoyed playing Tag in the park just like Keisha and I had done when we were younger. He was fast and I knew that day he was letting me win- like he did every other day. I raced up the wooden steps over to the bridge, which swayed from my weight as I headed towards the highest, curviest slide. I flung myself down the slide, the sound of the chains rattling as he crossed the bridge, chasing me. He caught me by surprise, flying down the smaller slide and meeting me at the bottom of mine.

"You're it!" he said excitedly, tagging me softly on my shoulder. I giggled and started chasing him again. We were teens but it felt good to act like little kids.

The happy memory transformed into the negative one. The one I avoided. The one that Mom avoided. The one that forced me into months of therapy.

A different park. Flashes of his fake smiles, greasy words, and re-jected pleas tumbled into my mind. I closed my eyes tightly, trying to squeeze it out of my brain. I found no peace from the images. I opened my eyes and reached for my cell phone on the nightstand next to the bed. I hit the video call option.

"Hey, girl!" Keisha's smiling face wiped away the ickiness that had contaminated my mind. "Why are you sitting in the dark?" Her voice held the facetiousness that always made me feel better. I chuckled and got up to flip the switch for the overhead light.

"Sorry, girl. I was just looking at the moon. It's full tonight."

"Oh. You've only been in Tiwa a week or so and you're already on your witch shit," Keisha said with a laugh.

I hopped back on the bed, sat cross-legged, and met Keisha's eyes through the phone. I smiled widely. Seeing my friend's face was always a relief. Not just because of her beautifully- nearly artistic- make up which enhanced her almond-shaped eyes, bell pepper nose, and full lips. It was the kindness in Keisha's eyes that always provided me with relief and allowed me to be vulnerable and open.

"Ha ha. You know Tiwans aren't witches and wizards," I said.

"I know, I know," Keisha laughed. "But I can't wrap my head around it. How do you do magic and you're not a witch?" she asked.

"I don't know. I can't explain it yet. I still have a lot to learn. The books don't do this place justice. It's all so different...but familiar."

"Familiar? Do you remember being there before? How old were you when you left?" Keisha placed her phone down and I could only see a white wall or ceiling. "I'm getting ready to go out, but I can hear you."

"I haven't been able to get anything from Mom." My voice lowered. "She's been sick almost since the moment we got here."

"Sick?" Keisha picked the phone back up and had a mascara wand in her other hand. "What's wrong with her?"

How much should I tell her? I shrugged back at the phone. "I don't know. I was out with friends today because she was feeling better. When I got home, she was asleep, so I didn't bother her."

Keisha put the wand down and focused. "You already made friends? What?! Tell me about them."

I described meeting Teddy at the festival and then at school. I told Keisha how Loreen was standoffish but it felt like she was starting to open up. I couldn't contain my excitement when describing the park. I paced around the room as I spoke about the bubbles and greenness of it all. "It reminded me about when we used to play at all the parks Mom would take us to. Then I started thinking about him. When he and I used to play at the park...after you left."

"Moved," Keisha corrected. "My parents moved."

"Right. Moved. I just started thinking about how things changed so much. After...The times I couldn't write because all I could do was think. Think about the what ifs. What if you had never moved? What if he was never my friend? What if? What if? What if? Then I would just freeze in the what was. How he took my power, stepped on my pride, and shit on my spirit."

I inhaled.

Keisha inhaled. "And now? How are you now?"

I exhaled. She knew I just needed to get it out. "I'm good now. Talking with you helps. I think Mom keeping her secrets is bringing up old feelings for me."

Keisha nodded. "I think you should keep trying to talk to her when she feels better. I would have never thought Ms. Brena would keep something like this from you. Tiwa is your heritage and you had no idea you were from there. Girl, I have so many questions so I know you have more."

"I will. I mean, I do have a lot of questions. Especially, why would she keep this from me? It doesn't make sense that she would hide anything from me."

"Well, maybe it does," Keisha said.

"What do you mean?"

"She doesn't talk about your dad. You don't even ask anymore."

"That's true." I traced the lines on the wooden floor with my toes. It had been years since I'd asked anything about my dad because Mom had been so unwilling to talk about it.

"So, this Teddy guy," Keisha changed the subject, "it sounds like he's interested." Her voice was flat and knowing.

"Maybe. But, you know..."

"I know."

Silence hung between us like an old friend that didn't mind being the third wheel. We sat comfortably in it. I followed the line of the black wooden plank to the off red baseboards. I could feel Keisha watching me through the phone.

"How's the apartment?" she asked. "Give me a tour."

The wooden floor creaked from the weight of my body as I got up from the bed. I turned the camera to face the room and started with the large armoire that was placed on the wall opposite the door. "There's no closet here, but this was here when we moved and so far, it holds most of my clothes...if I don't buy anymore."

We giggled in unison.

"So, you'll need more storage space soon. At least when you're ready to start back dressing like you used to and not the baggy clothes," Keisha said.

I nodded. I continued the tour with the large wooden desk that sat against the wall opposite the door and ended with the queen-sized bed on the same wall as the door. I pointed the camera at the window to share the moon.

Keisha nodded as if in acceptance of the room. A knock rapped on my door, interrupting our conversation. I faced the sound. "Show me the rest," Keisha said. I stood motionless in front of the door. I had that strange feeling again. The knock repeated louder. Keisha heard it this time. "Hey, it's your mom. Let me say hi."

I couldn't move. I looked from the phone to the door, hoping it was Mom on the other side. Something told me it probably wasn't. I knew Keisha would believe anything I told her but I didn't know if I, myself, believed what I'd seen in the building. I almost felt crazy for thinking it wasn't Mom knocking.

"Maybe later," I said, trying to hide the tremble in my voice. "You know how she gets about people seeing her when she thinks she looks crazy."

I knew Keisha understood me well enough to hear everything I left unsaid and tried to hide from her. I knew she wouldn't ask. I knew my friend would let me talk about it when I was ready.

"Yea, so true." Keisha smiled. "Ok, friend. Later."

"Later. We'll talk soon?"

"You know it!" Keisha waved and disconnected the call.

The knock begged for me to answer.

"Hey-" I said. I pulled my bedroom door open to find an empty moonlit hallway.

11

I stepped carefully into the dimly lit hallway. The light from the fixture overhead was absorbed into the wall and stretched into darkness. "I hate how creepy this place gets at night," I said. There was no comfort in hearing my own voice as it bounced off the walls. The sound of my footsteps on the hardwood floor reverberated into a tiny echo through the vaulted ceilings. The noises distracted me from thinking about the knock on my door.

Mom's bedroom door gave a long, slow creek when I pressed against it. The nightlight under her bed formed a halo around the headboard, cradling the top half of the bed in a soft glow. I approached her quietly, squinting to improve my vision in the dark. Her blanket had been tossed off to the side. I inspected the shape and curve of her body. The hair on the back of my neck stood up.

Mom's legs lay flat and towards the left edge of the bed with her knees slightly bent. Like some ghostly yoga pose, her abdomen and chest were held contorted in the air, her elbows bent but inches off the bed. I shrieked at the sight of her neck lifted in strain and her throat bulging as she hovered above the pillow. Her face was pulled back in a grimace, her eyes open...vacant...seeing nothing.

"What..." I moved closer to the bed. Her chest rose and fell in shallow movements. I fumbled with my phone. With clarity I didn't know I possessed, I located the number Teddy had given me for the Helper Clinic. Keeping an eye on Mom's body, I hit the call button. My jaw was clenched so tightly it almost hurt. Each ring felt like a lifetime.

"Helper Clinic. Ba wo ni?" the voice sang from the phone.

"My mother. My mother needs help," I managed to vocalize. "She's not able to respond to me. I can't tell what's going on. She's just staring. And her body..." My voice trailed off.

"Where is the current place of the emergency?" the voice replied, calm and firm.

I gave the address I had reviewed time and time again before the move. It felt like ages ago when I was trying to make sense of Mom and I moving from Chicago to Tiwa. That I was really from... "Tiwa," I puffed at the end of my address.

"Will you repeat that address?" the voice asked. I tuned back to the conversation. The tone of the voice from the other side of the phone changed from helpful to almost antagonistic. I thought I also sensed some trepidation in the voice. I repeated the address and matched the calm and firmness I initially received from the Helper.

"One moment," the voice said.

I turned away from Mom in search of a spot and focused on her altar to remain calm. The strangers in the photos looking back at me served that purpose.

"Apologies, ma'am," the voice said. "We don't currently have enough Helpers in the clinic to support a transport. There will be a wait."

"A wait?!" The southside Chicago part of me was popping up in my tone. "How. Long?" Everything I'd read about Tiwa and its health-care system indicated services were provided promptly and at little to no expense to those in need. Indignation swelled like a dark cloud in my chest.

"One moment," the voice replied.

I glanced at the phone, watching the seconds tick away. The voice returned to the phone and I unclenched my fists.

"Three hours, ma'am," the voice replied.

I blurted out every curse word and scathing phrase that I could think of. "Look, got damnit. My mother needs support *now* and you will have transport here A. S. got damn A. P.! If something happens to her, you and the rest of Ibeji Village will have to see me!"

"One moment," the voice replied. I sent a silent scream to the ceiling. Although it felt like hours, the voice returned within a couple of moments. "Transport will arrive within the next ten minutes. Keep your phone near you in case further information is either requested or provided."

I acknowledged, ended the call, and returned to Mom's bedside. She had not changed her position. I couldn't understand how it was possible for her to be held up like that. I found solace that she continued to breathe while being severely contorted…and held in the air.

"They're coming to help, Mom." I fought the urge to go to her bedside and touch her to comfort her. It didn't feel safe to do. Whose safety I was worried about? Mine or hers?

My phone rang after a few minutes. A different voice was on the other side. "Ba wo ni? This is the Helper Clinic. We are outside the building. Is it possible for the patient to come outside? We are ready to meet her."

I pulled the phone away from my ear and stared at it in disbelief. I replayed the earlier conversation in my mind and was confident I'd given the correct information about Mom's condition. I rubbed my temple.

"No. She cannot," I replied.

Another pause.

"We weren't given complete information about the situation. We're on our way up," the voice advised.

* * *

"She's back here," I gestured, holding the apartment door open for the two Helpers and a tiny white dog. They hesitated before crossing the threshold. Even the white dog hung back, following his owner's lead without any verbal commands. "Over. Here," I commanded as I headed down the hall towards Mom's room. The two Helpers- men, one taller than the other- each wore short locs as if the hairstyle was a part of the uniform, along with the black and white jackets labeled "Helper" and black bags they carried. All of them trailed far behind me, reluctantly led to the back of the apartment. I heard the patter of the tiny dog's feet following behind the shorter Helper.

Mom's body had eased into a more natural state on the bed. Her locs hung over the pillow as if framed aesthetically around her sleeping face. Her arms laid relaxed at the side of her body. Her chest and abdomen lay fully flat on the bed. The blanket that had previously been tossed to the side now covered her. "I-." My mind raced with theories about how she got into her current position. "She wasn't like this before," I stammered. "Her body was cont-"

The taller of the two Helpers stepped up to the bedside while opening his bag. "Ma'am?" He gently touched Mom's shoulder. "What's her name?" He spoke to me without eye contact, instead focusing on the task at hand.

"Brena. Her name is Brena." I clutched my hands to my chest and stepped away from the Helpers. The dog hopped on the bed next to Mom and lay its head next to hers on the pillow. Was it checking her like the Helpers did? Was the dog a Helper? I wasn't the type for dogs on the bed, but I was so confused I didn't comment.

The taller Helper leaned closer to her. "Brena. My name is Will. My partner, Reg, and I will be taking care of you today." No response. "Reg," Will called out to his partner.

I loosened up when I saw the two working in tandem to get her pulse, check her blood pressure, and make a clinical decision about what they were seeing. They made no acknowledgement of me repeating how I had found her. Reg called out that he'd be back with the stretcher. The dog hopped off the bed and followed behind him.

"We're taking her to the clinic," Will advised, still avoiding eye contact. His attention was on the notes he was making on his tablet. "There's only so much we can do here. We have Healers in the clinic that will be able to better diagnose and treat her."

I nodded, my hands still tight across my chest. "I want to come."

Will put the notebook away and stared at his partner who returned with the stretcher. He gave no indication he'd heard me while he helped Reg get the stretcher into position. The dog hadn't returned.

The Helpers moved quickly to stabilize Mom and get her positioned on the stretcher. I moved out of the way. I realized I hadn't even thought of the knocking that had occurred before finding her catatonic. Fear crawled up my spine as I thought about being alone in the apartment, in this strange village, in this foreign land.

"I want to come," I said again, louder this time. Will finally made eye contact, giving me a look filled with empathy and reluctance as he and Reg positioned themselves to wheel Mom out of the room. Out of the apartment. To leave me by myself.

"Look, I get it. I'd love to have time to discuss this with you further, but..." he paused, looking at the room, a shudder escaping his body, "we have to go." Reg began pulling the stretcher out of the room. Will pushed while he kept speaking. "You'll have to stay here. You can call the same number you first called in about thirty minutes to check on the status of your mother and learn about the next steps."

I followed them down the hall, out the door, and to the elevator. "I don't understand. This is my mother. I need to be with her." I was almost whining. Why did I have to beg? Reg and Will looked impatiently at the display on the elevator, letting them know it was on its way. Will sighed.

"Normal protocol is that the patient is checked in before any family can come." I noticed Reg glance from the elevator and raise an eyebrow at his partner. Was he telling the truth? "You can call in thirty minutes to check on her. Now, we have to go," Will finished. The ding of the elevator ended the discussion. I felt comfortable enough to kiss Mom's forehead as they rolled her onto it.

Will held the door as Reg made sure Mom was in safely. He looked directly at me. "It's none of my business, Miss. But maybe you should think of...of not staying here." He shook his head slowly as the elevator doors began to close. "You need a long spoon to dine with the devil," he said as the doors shut. Leaving me staring at them, confused.

12

Then

Even with the curtains drawn tightly, the relentless sun blazes into the room, its searing rays piercing through the narrow cracks of the expansive windows. The girl kneels on the soft bedspread next to her mother, her fingers tracing the clammy, perspiring palm that she holds tightly. The room is filled with the scent of sweat mingled with the faint aroma of lavender air freshener, a feeble attempt to mask the heaviness in the air.

She studies her mother, her eyes traveling from where they are connected at her mother's soft yet withered hand up towards the dark circles and slight creases near her closed eyes. Even in her sickly state, her mother appears peaceful. Her long coily hair is strewn about the pillow with tiny tendrils plastered in sweat beads around the thinning structure of her face. The girl thinks that sitting here in the bed- away from her father's commands and his needs- her mother is in the most peaceful state she's probably ever been in. She is aware of how frail her mother looks in the bed, swallowed by too many pillows and a bundle of bedding. She chooses to focus on the good memories. These are what she shares with her sleeping mother. The girl speaks and watches her mother's eyelids flutter. It's easy to believe that the flutters are responses to her stories. Pleasure in revisiting the memories.

The girl reminds her mother of the time the family visited the mainland. What was supposed to be a business trip for her father turned into a family vacation. It was one of the only times the girl could remember her mother standing up to her father. The girl shares how proud she was when her mother had demanded that her father show them around the Bay Area of California and not leave them in the hotel for the day again. The girl retells how much fun she had seeing the Nutcracker in San Francisco then heading to FAO Schwarz where she had her pick of all the toys she wanted. She leaves out the argument. There's no need to share what she overheard later that evening. But she remembers it all the same.

Her father wanted to return to work and send them back to Tiwa without him. Her mother wanted to complete the trip as a family. They argued in the suite, maybe unaware that she could hear them from her room. Maybe they didn't care. She knew it wouldn't bother her father if he knew she could hear. She knows she should not mention the loud slap and her mother's agonizing scream after her mother accused her father of wanting to spend time with his "San Francisco woman." She remembers clearly how her father confirmed the suspicions before he slammed the door in her mother's crying, bleeding face. The girl only shares the happiness she felt in feeling like a family, even if it was fleeting.

A cloud passes over the sun, shrouding the room in darkness. The girl sighs when she hears the sound of her father's footsteps coming down the hallway, his heavy hand opening the door as he enters. She continues with her story. She describes the private plane ride from San Francisco to Knoxville, TN- almost a few hours drive from the Tiwa border- and how much she enjoyed it. Seeing all the mainlanders and observing the similarities and differences from Tiwans. Passing through the borders and hearing the murmured chants of the Prayer Helpers. She leaves out the details about her father's stony silence during the car ride from the airport through the Tiwa entrance and all the way home.

The girl glances up at her father, hoping to find a flicker of understanding or compassion in his eyes, but all she sees is confusion and detachment. His face remains a mask, concealing the depth of his own emotions or lack thereof. He has never demonstrated understanding of the bond between her and her mother. He doesn't understand how a person can get sick from a broken heart. The Helpers from the clinic have told the girl and her father that her mother- his wife-suffers from acute stress that has led to heart failure. He does not understand, as his daughter does, that he is the cause of the stress. From his denial of affection, autonomy, and acceptance of his wife of over fifteen years.

The girl focuses back on her mother, grateful that she has another happy memory to share. She tells her tale as if her father isn't standing over them and watching them with the mild contempt that has always filled any room he enters.

The girl feels her mother's hand go limp. Her mother's breathing becomes increasingly labored as the girl tells her stories, her words punctuated by moments of fluttering eyelids, as if her mother is momentarily transported into the memories. But as the girl reaches the end of her tale, a chilling silence settles upon the room. It is then that the girl places her head gently on her mother's chest, searching for the familiar rhythm of her heartbeat, only to be met with an empty stillness.

"She's gone," he says in the way he always says things- devoid of emotion. "You have until the Helpers come to say your goodbyes." He huffs as he checks his watch, his action betraying his eagerness to resume the efficiency of his routine, oblivious to the devastation that engulfs his daughter. "I called them before I came in. They should be here any moment." He leaves and closes the door behind him. The clouds part from the sun, casting out most of the darkness in the room.

Her head remains on her mother's chest, understanding the callousness in her father's comment but not reacting to it. She learned long ago that reacting changed nothing. No child should lose their mother at eleven, but especially his child. A sharp pain stabs her in the chest. She can feel her heart breaking. For the loss of her mother, the loss of her advocate, and the loss of any freedom she had left.

13

Saturday

I used to enjoy my chores. I found them relaxing and a way to distract myself from my thoughts. Weekend mornings had been bonding times for Mom and me. We would play our favorite music and work together to get the apartment cleaned. Washing the dishes, drying them, and putting them away provided me with solace. Sweeping and vacuuming were mindless and rhythmic enough to help clear my head. Having a clean space always felt therapeutic. Until today.

Today, I preferred the silence over a song that would remind me of Mom's absence. She'd only been gone overnight. When I'd called to confirm that she was checked in, the Helpers informed me they were monitoring her and they'd be in contact if anything changed. Or, maybe later today after some test results came back. I felt guilty that I wasn't staying at the Helper Clinic with her, but they reassured me that there wasn't anything I could do. The Helper on the phone told me I could visit once some of the test results came back. I had resolved to get the apartment into a livable space with the boxes unpacked, and everything in its place before Mom came home...whenever that would be.

I'd awakened that morning full of purpose and hope. Opening all the curtains in the living room, kitchen, and my bedroom brightened up the apartment. My usual breakfast of a veggie omelet and a cup of green tea filled my belly and eased my spirits. I enjoyed each bite and all the flavors that played across my tongue. I avoided thinking about all the food Mom had left untouched when she fell sick. I stayed in the moment.

After enjoying the meal while reading one of my textbooks, *The Rebellion of 1842 and Tiwa*, I cleaned up the breakfast dishes and wiped down the counters. "Mop...where's the mop?" I asked a mother that wasn't there.

I found the mop and bucket in the pantry with other cleaning supplies and food staples. After adding a cleaning solution and Florida water- just as Mom had taught me- I took the bucket to the kitchen sink and turned on the faucet. Nothing came out. Turning the knob off and then on again didn't help. The pipes didn't even make a sound to indicate the water was coming like they had done in my old apartment. I tried the off-again-on-again technique. A noise sounded from the pipe, sans the water. I removed the bucket from the sink and held my long braids away from my ear as I leaned down closer to the sink to hear. The noise was faint but it grew louder. I bent down further, leaning in as close as I could get to hear more clearly. I thought I heard a voice.

I held my breath, listening intently to the hole in the sink. A man's voice rose to my ear. I leaned in a micro fraction of an inch closer. "I know I'm not crazy," I whispered. The previously incoherent voice came through the pipe more clearly.

"I'm here."

I jumped back just in time to miss being wet by the water that splashed down from the faucet. I watched the water go down the drain. Something else was going to happen. Maybe the voice would turn into smoke. Maybe the smoke would turn into some apparition. I tried not to let my imagination get the best of me. It seemed safe for the moment. The water flowed in its natural state, out of the faucet and into the sink. I filled the bucket.

Although I missed more than a few spots, I got through mopping the kitchen pretty quickly. Nothing else came out of the drain after I poured the dirty water in the sink. I felt okay to clean the rest of the apartment.

The living room didn't take much time at all. A quick sweep of the hardwood floors and some dusting and I was done. I closed my eyes and sighed with relief. So far, so good. A nagging feeling started to well up inside of me, but I still had the bathroom to do. Once I did, I would be done. I examined the supplies and imagined pulling it off without any peculiarities.

The bath, toilet, sink, and counters were a breeze. No issues wiping them down. The water flowed fine. I even paused while cleaning the sink to give space to any voices that wanted to be heard. Nothing.

My final task for the afternoon was the bathroom mirror. My arms swiped up and down, removing streaks and grime. Up and down. Up and down. After a couple swipes, I saw that my reflection wasn't wiping along with me. It stood still with its hands hanging at its side. Watching me. I stopped and took a step back, cautious of my reflection. Where I had long, clean braids, I could see gnats flying around and worms inside its frizzy braids through the mirror. It smirked at me sinisterly as it walked closer to the counter.

Keeping my eye on the mirror, I started walking backwards. The mirror's image continued moving forward. I nearly stumbled into the clawfoot tub. My reflection reached out to the sink, its elongated, skinny hands with long, brittle sharp nails reaching out of the sides of the mirror. It pulled its body up. Half of it was now on the outside of the mirror. I couldn't move. I watched as its whole body crawled out of the mirror and crouched on top of the counter. The pungent smell of decay filled my nose. The way the reflection moved, without sound, filled the bathroom with an eerie silence. It moved its head slowly, tilting it menacingly as it studied me with its jaundiced eyes.

I was frozen. The door to the bathroom was open and if I moved now, I could reach it without worry that my reflection would touch me. Goosebumps covered my arms, prickly along with my raised hair. My reflection widened its mouth to smile, revealing layers of yellowed, rotting, sharp, jagged teeth. It hissed noiselessly at me.

The air was heavy with my fear and the menacing motivations of the creature in front of me. I tried stepping back again, only to fall into the tub, pulling at the shower curtain for balance. The curtain rings snapped off the oval-shaped pole and the curtain draped over me. My arms flailed through the plastic, trying to get free from under it and out of the tub, to escape the threatening version of myself. The rustling and my grunts were not loud enough to cover the slither my reflection was now making on the tile floor as it moved closer. I screamed. The slithering sound grew closer. I was nearly free. I threw the curtain to the side, expecting my reflection to be on top of me. Instead, the room was empty.

I was alone.

I ran. Out of the bathroom. Out of the apartment. From the building and down several streets for good measure.

14

The rain was an old and welcome friend to me. It held and cuddled me through the warm afternoon while I walked the streets of Ibeji Village. I was reminded of the hot Chicago summer days when I had sat on friends' stoops, watching the heat emanate from the sidewalk. The rain had quickly evaporated after barely touching the ground. I wished I could evaporate. Disappear. Not to anywhere in particular. Just to another place where Mom was with me instead of at some Helper Clinic. Where I was with friends and I wasn't alone in a strange land I didn't know enough about. A place where monster reflections weren't hopping out of mirrors.

I was fine not having my umbrella. It was like the rain provided me cover from other potential monstrosities. It wasn't like I was going back to the apartment. Not for an umbrella, anyway. Instead, I found cover under awnings and trees, whatever was available on my journey to nowhere in particular.

Streetlights came on and guided me as I traveled down Victoria Avenue, a right on Bloom Street, and another right on Clarion Street. Reading the street signs empowered me, like I had focus. I treaded slowly. The afternoon had transitioned into night. The shops were either closing or closed. Most Ibejians were at home with their families, friends, or ancestors. I was grateful to be alone with the sounds of rain and the infrequent splash of my foot in a puddle.

I found myself standing in front of a 24-hour bookstore. *Maybe you need to be around more people*, I thought to myself. I went in.

Inside, a bright light showed a few people who didn't want to be with their family, friends, or ancestors alone. Reading alongside the strangers would be a good distraction.

* * *

"Late night, Ms. Bennett?"

I lifted my head from the back of a book to the smiling face of an old woman with a tiny afro cropped close to her head. She was about my height, taller than most women. She was dressed in grey sweatpants, a black t-shirt, and a long floral silk-like robe. There was a familiarity about her I couldn't place. I eyed the makeup caked on her face and tried to return her smile.

"Excuse me?" I replied. How did she know my name?

"Oh, I'm sorry," she started, her Tiwa accent heavy and dripping with sweetness. "I'm Ellie. I live in Yardley Place. I saw your name on some of your boxes when the Helpers were moving you and your mother in. Are you ok? You looked upset coming in."

I put the book I was looking at back on the shelf. Was this lady following me? "I'm fine. Thank you." I tried to remain respectful since she was my elder.

"Ah. Well, good. Now, are you Brena or Imani?"

I lifted one eyebrow.

"Oh, well the boxes had both names. Hard to tell who is who," she laughed. Her laugh sparkled and put me more at ease. Hadn't I come into the bookstore to be around more people?

"I'm Imani. And I'm ok. Just needed to get out of the house for a bit. Be around people."

Ellie nodded. "I understand. I was just leaving the bookstore to head back to my place. I can wait and walk back home with you. If you'd like." Her offer felt genuine, like she really wanted to help me.

I turned back to the shelves and pretended to look at the titles. If she didn't live in Yardley Place, would it be safe to go back with her? She already knew I lived there. She probably even knew what apartment number. The image of the grisly version of me chasing me out of the mirror solidified my decision.

I looked back at her. "Sure. I wasn't going to buy anything. I was just looking. We can go now."

Ellie smiled. For a microsecond, her smile brought the reflection to mind. Tonight's events affected me more than I realized. I shook off the image and walked with her out of the store.

15

The rain had stopped and the night remained warm. We meandered back to Yardley Place. Ellie was pleasant. I was brave enough to ask her about the building and if she'd seen anything strange there.

"Strange?" she asked. "One might call all of Tiwa strange. Especially someone from the mainland. What do you mean by strange?" Her question was pointed.

"How'd you know?" She knew I was from the mainland. Something else suspicious?

"You still haven't greeted me in the traditional manner, Ms. Imani."

How embarrassing. "It's something I haven't gotten used to all the way."

"Mmhm. It's forgiven." She waved her hand in the air, her rings glistening in the lamplight. A silver snake ring wrapped around her right index finger caught my eye. Its singular eye shimmered blue green when it caught the light. "You can make it up to me though."

"Oh?"

We'd made it inside the lobby of Yardley Place and she was pointing towards a first-floor apartment. "You look like you need a good meal. Come to my apartment. Let's eat."

My stomach rumbled on cue.

"Sure. I could eat." I shrugged.

Ellie's home in apartment 1B was bare. The walls were void of any paintings or portraits. There was no couch or other living room furniture. The only things I saw was the kitchen table with two chairs. *She probably sleeps on a mattress on the floor*, I chuckled to myself.

"I just got back into the I.V.," Ellie said as if she read my mind. "Just before you and your mother did. Still waiting on the rest of my furniture to arrive. Have a seat. I'm gonna start some jollof rice." She headed into her kitchen.

I followed her. "I can help," I said. I took the onions she had sitting on her counter. "Where's your knife and cutting board?"

"O! Your mother taught you how to make jollof rice?"

I couldn't grasp the tone of her words. There was something underlying their affability. The cold nagging feeling blew through my body. I dismissed the feeling, grinned, and focused on the work at hand.

"But to answer your question, Miss Imani~"

"My question?" I wiped some of the tears that were streaming down my cheeks. I should have rinsed the onions under cold water.

"About strange things in this building. I've heard about them, too. Tiwa is filled with magic and ancestors and lore which can lead to a ghost story here and there. There's been a few about Yardley Place. But, keep in mind, most haunted house stories in Tiwa actually end up being the ancestors of the 'haunted' trying to help their hard-headed kin. Not a true haunting. Not like what you may have heard about from the mainland. Yet, still, the stories grow and it affects how people act around the building." She sighed. It must've been hard to overcome all the tales created in the mainland about Tiwa. Like how Teddy and Loreen believed everything they heard about Chicago.

"Like the people from the Helper Clinic," I muttered.

"What do you mean?" She moved on from chopping celery to chopping carrots. I pushed the onions I'd chopped from the edge of the counter towards the black and red checkered backdrop of her other counter. I leaned against the counter and recounted my experience with the Helper Clinic and their reluctance to help.

"So, Brena is sick?" She said it in that tone I still couldn't place. A familiarity that almost seemed unwarranted. "I'm sorry to hear that."

"Yes. Almost as soon as we got here," I said.

"That sounds about right. With the Helper Clinic, I mean." She started sautéing the vegetables. She looked at me and I felt comfort from her again. "That doesn't mean that the building is haunted though. It's just superstition, young lady. A coincidence that your mom got sick."

"You think so?" I cleaned and diced the chicken she pushed my way.

"Yes, Imani. A coincidence."

We finished cooking together, working in tandem in the kitchen. When the meal was completed, we sat at the unclothed table and enjoyed our food while talking about topics unrelated to the scariness of the building. I talked about my writing and things I wanted to accomplish in Tiwa.

"Do you have anything I can read?" she'd asked.

"No," I said between bites. "I haven't written in a couple of years."

She regarded me with curiosity. "Not inspired?"

I shrugged. "I guess," I said. I still didn't know this lady. She didn't need to know that I'd felt like my words, among other things, were stolen from me a couple of years ago. "But, I've felt more inspired since we moved."

She smiled and changed the subject. We finished our meal with small talk about the weather in Tiwa, the Ibeji Village Festival of the Family, and my classes. Anything to keep my mind off the strangeness of the building.

I left her home feeling fed by her food and her company. I returned to my apartment in peace.

16

The place was quiet. Fatigue settled into my mind and body. Being tired was a superpower in this home. When sleep was my only focus, I had less anxiety around strange things happening. There was less opportunity for me to experience them. My dreams were safe from the stress of reality and I was looking forward to them. A quick shower would be the best way to relax and wind all the way down. After the meal and conversation with Ellie, it felt safe.

I'd gotten in the habit of turning on all the lights when the sun was starting to set and keeping most of them on through the night. Tonight was no different. I walked into the well-lit bathroom, avoiding my reflection in the mirror, and turned on the shower. I stopped as I was about to remove my t-shirt.

The smell of morning glory filled my nostrils. *Move legs*, I thought to myself. Nothing happened. I tried to yell *MOVE LEGS*, but the scream only happened in my head. I could not move my legs...until they did move.

My body turned to the mirror that was quickly fogging up with shower steam. My reflection matched my actions. Relief was brief. My face was ashen. My body stood unnaturally stiff and my heart beat rapidly and quickly against my chest. I was starting to accept that I no longer had control over my body and, yet, somewhat grateful that I still had control over my mind. *This is different from what happened to my mom*, I thought to myself. *I'm still awake. I'm still aware. Maybe I can get control of my body back.*

My body did not respond to my attempts to move. Instead, it walked me out of the bathroom and towards the front door. My hand reached for and turned the doorknob. My legs walked me out of the apartment. I screamed inside of my mind as I was walked towards the lobby of the apartment building. *Please let someone see me. Please let someone be able to help me. Ellie!*

I felt like a baby doll being moved through the dollhouse at the whim of a petulant child. I was stopped in the middle of the lobby. I put all my energy into making my head turn towards Ellie's apartment. My body refused to respond. I twilled my mouth to scream her name. Nothing. Helplessness set in my bones.

The night lighting from the overhead chandeliers threw shadows all over the empty room. A slight breeze from an unknown source slightly shook the chandeliers, making the shadows appear to dance on the wall. My heart bounced against my chest, threatening to pop out. I tried to use the breathing techniques that had helped me in the past but couldn't even control the rate of my breathing. I had no control of any part of my body except my mind. *Relax, Imani. Relax.*

The invisible force turned my body in a circle around the lobby, my head bobbing up and down, as if the imaginary child had me searching for something. When it didn't find what it was looking for, my legs were slightly bent to march me up the stairs to the second-floor apartments. I secretly wished I could grab the railing. The weight of my upper body leaned unnaturally far back while my legs traveled up the stairs and my arms hung limply at my side. Finally, with the acceptance that I was no longer in control of anything, at the top of the stairs, I found the ability to relax my mind.

I was danced by the invisible force, passing the row of apartments that were on the left side of the building. As I began to slow down, I realized I was not being taken into my apartment. I was stopping in front of apartment 8B, facing it square on. No light could be seen coming from under the door and the apartment was quiet. If I could have moved, I would have run back to my apartment, into my bedroom, shut the door, and stayed under the covers until morning. But the unseen force held me there for a long moment before it hiked me towards the end of the hall.

17

Sunday

I stirred. The cement was cold on my face. Muscles I'd never worked out before ached. The smell of garbage floated in my nose. I sat up slowly to take in my surroundings. The basement. Judging by the dim light coming through the small windows near the ceiling, the sun had just barely risen. I used the large composition bin to steady myself and get up from the floor. *I was dropped off like the garbage.* I positioned myself to stand. A quick inspection of my body revealed no injuries. Just the stiffness of various joints and muscles that could be soothed by a nice warm bath. Or shower.

A shower. I pondered the events that had led me here. Being forced out of my home to walk around the building, not able to control any part of my body. I had no recollection of being taken into the basement. Yet that's where I was left. My heart started racing again. I had to make it to my apartment before something decided to hold me hostage as a doll again.

I didn't run into anyone- or anything- from the basement back to my home. I dallied inside the apartment, listening for anything strange. Aside from the running shower, it was silent. Daylight filled every corner. I rushed into the bathroom and turned off the shower. Fear was becoming my constant companion. Joining me at every turn, persistent and unabating. The bathroom did not seem a safe place. There'd be no shower right now. Sleep was more important than a warm bath. I didn't have class for a few more hours, so an early morning nap would set me in the right mood.

The bed felt good. The blanket was comforting and the pillow gently soothed most of the fear and stress from my brain. I still couldn't sleep though. Anxiety joined up with fear as my new playmate. What if I woke up somewhere outside of the building? Somewhere far and outside what I knew of Tiwa? What if my body was taken over again, but permanently this time? I didn't know enough people to be able to get help. My thoughts raced about all the things that could go wrong if something else happened. There'd be no sleep either.

I thought about calling Teddy. Could he help me? Could I trust him? He seemed to be knowledgeable about Ibeji Village. My head crinkled the pillow as I shook it "no." I couldn't call Teddy. I didn't know him like that. I didn't trust him.

What about Loreen? I giggled to myself. Immediate no. That lady did not like me and I wasn't going to kiss anybody's butt to get answers. Even if it meant getting help.

I got up and pulled out my laptop to search for anything I could find about the building. I started with the Yardleys. There were multiple articles about their role in founding Ibeji Village. Even some with pictures of Raymond Yardley and of the other founders. I tried to find any personal information about Raymond, his family, or the building. After an hour of searching, I was getting frustrated. There wasn't anything else to be found about Raymond or his family. Not even pictures. Nothing about his personal history. And not a word about the potential haunting of the house. Nothing except an article about Raymond's unexpectant disappearance nearly twenty years ago- around the time I was born. I excused anxiety and fear and let hope in. This was a start.

18

Then

The little girl has grown into a teenager. She is nearly the spitting image of her mother, except with the beauty of youth. Her face is smooth and flawless, her eyes wide with a fading innocence. Her shape has evolved to more resemble a woman's, her clothes filled out with puberty. Her long coily hair is pulled into a neat, low bun with a part in the middle. She stands in the middle of her father's office, asking for his attention. He avoids her, unable to deny the resemblance between her and her mother. He remains focused on the work in front of him.

"Dad," she calls to him, again. "I want to get out of this house. Can't I go shopping, hang out with kids my own age? I'm tired of only being with the help." Her voice is steady and calm. She learned long ago that showing emotion was a weakness to him, a deterrence to getting her needs met. Her tone stays even. She speaks plainly. "I've followed your rules as you asked. I listen to the tutor. She said I'm doing well with my studies. Can't I just get out of the house for an afternoon? Maybe we can do something together?" She nearly regrets the desperation in her final question. She remains hopeful since she hasn't shared that she feels trapped inside a living coffin, unable to escape the memories of her mother or nightmares of her father.

A single grunt escapes her father's lips. That will be the extent of his response. The levee holding back her emotions is crumbling. She steps forward. Right up to and in front of the desk. She waves her hand in front of his computer screen. She swishes through the papers that sit loose on his desk. She shouts to get his attention. "Daddy!" The girl stalks around the desk and twirls his chair to face her. For what feels like the millionth time, she repeats her requests.

His face is blank, detached from her explosion. He rolls his chair back, stands, and reaches for a ledger book from the shelves behind him. He returns to his work.

The levee holding back her emotions is falling. "I wish Momma were here. At least she knew I existed. At least she cared. You never cared. Not about me. Not about her," she says, her voice trembling with the last bit of indifference she can hold onto.

He hears her and meets his daughter's gaze. To him, the ghost of his dead wife haunts him from a child's tantrum. He views her childish attempt as proof that she does not belong out in the world, shaming his name, causing him distractions. He has no intention of giving her what she asks for.

"Get out," he says firmly and unkindly.

Her mouth drops open. She closes it as she comes to understand the futility of her behavior. Nothing will ever change. She leaves his office. He doesn't respond after she slams the door behind her. She's not even worth the chiding.

The walls of the building feel like they are moving in closer, holding her captive. Suffocating her. She hurries down the long hallway to her room. She closes her door softly. The sound of another slammed door would make no difference to her father. He wouldn't be able to hear it while in his office, anyway. She's tired of futility.

She paces her cluttered room, avoiding all the books and clothing strewn about the floor. Her chest heaves with anger as tears run down her face. She picks up one of the dolls her mother bought her and examines it. She fingers the beautiful, short, yellow Ankara dress that covers the brown-skinned doll. She swings the doll around in a music-less dance. The dancing couple sashay around the room. The girl stops at her dresser and picks up a blue hair ribbon. She gives the doll the same smile her mother used to give her just before doing her hair. A smile full of tenderness and love. She begins winding the blue ribbon around the doll's shoulders, down its body, to where it ends at its feet. If the doll were a person, her limbs would have been bound from any movement. While the girl ties the two ends of the ribbon together, ensuring the doll's limbs stay in place, someone knocks at her door. After hiding the doll under her pillow, she lets in her guest.

The boy has also grown. The hair above his lip ages him some beyond his years, but his eyes still beam with youth and naivety. There has been no change in the adoration he feels when he sees her. Through all these years, he continues to be her faithful servant, following her every command. His face still widens with excitement and curiosity for their next interaction. He never knows what's next with her, but he always enjoys the journey. When she talks with him, the butterflies swirl in his stomach and his heart races in his chest. He relishes the moments when she is looking at him, wishing that she was closer to looking *at* him the way he looks at her, but aware of the loneliness and pain she is experiencing.

The pair sit together on the bed. He is careful to maintain the space between them. Should someone walk in, there should be no appearance of inappropriate behavior between the help and the mistress of the home.

"Are you okay?" His voice is gentle and filled with genuine empathy. Not the forced compassion she is used to hearing from the other Helpers in her home.

She doesn't respond right away. Instead, she resumes her pacing. She is almost annoyed by the longing that is draped around him like a coat, but her fury for her father is a stronger emotion. The anger swells within her and is released through a diatribe about how horrible her father is. "He never cared for her," she repeats as often as "He never cared for me."

She tries to describe the emptiness that has haunted her since her mother died but can't find the words. Nothing she says could conceptualize the constant desire for parental love and its constant denial. If she could share these feelings, maybe she could tread water instead of the darkness engulfing her spirit like water in her lungs. Instead, she shares how her father treated her mother like one of the other tacky objects he kept as a monument to his achievements. How he never saw how sick her mother was getting, tossing her to the side and never visiting either of them when her mother could no longer leave the bed. The girl's pacing around the room quickens, matching the ferocity of her rage.

But she does not yell. The boy notes that her voice is calm, her words specific and concise. He listens. He was there when her mother grew so frail that even his mother- also a Helper- could not coax her to eat. He witnessed when the girl took up residence in her mother's room. When she realized her mother was not going to get better, he felt her sadness. Even now he can feel her pain. He wants to take all that sorrow from her. He wants to take away her anger. The boy listens, but he does not speak. Who was he to interrupt? What did he have to add?

The girl declares vengeance and retribution. She wishes that her father could be on her ancestor table. Then she wishes that he wasn't. Her pacing slows as an idea grows within her. What if he wasn't on her ancestor table? What if he was never on her ancestor table?

The boy cocks his head sideways. He is both confused and curious. He waits for her to speak again. He waits for her idea to form and become a plan, something achievable. He waits for her to tell him what part he needs to play. He waits to tell her that he would do anything. Anything she needed.

19

Monday

"Alright students," Dr. Pike called out as she shut down the projector. "Your projects are due in three weeks. If you haven't found a partner or group, let me know so I can connect the lost with the lost," she guffawed.

My feet were as heavy as my heart. I shuffled past exiting students and empty seats, watching the floor as I headed to leave. Teddy must've noticed me. He was waiting just outside the door. What did he want?

"Ms. Bennett, a moment, jowo," Dr. Pike called out.

I raised my head at the sound of my name and nodded. The floor became interesting again, just until I met Dr. Pike at the podium.

"Ba wo ni, angel? Get any sleep recently?" Dr. Pike finished packing her belongings and zipped up her bag.

I didn't want to speak. Tears, anger, and fear waited at the periphery to escape if I opened my mouth. I could only nod in response to her.

Dr. Pike remained unusually quiet. I felt her studying me and matched her silence. "How have you been acclimating to Tiwa?" she finally asked.

I shrugged slightly, trying to hide my fear, my guilt. I was so overwhelmed by all the strange things happening in my home, I hadn't returned the message the Helper Clinic had left. They were letting me know my mother was doing well. Mom would be okay. She was under the care of a good medical team. My priority was the apartment. I wanted to tell Dr. Pike about the strange things in the building.

I lifted my head to meet her concerned look. "I live in Yardley Place. And there's something wrong with my apartment, Dr. Pike. Something is wrong with the whole building," I managed to get out. I watched her face closely and saw awareness creep in.

"Yardley Place?" the professor asked.

"Yes. Does that mean anything to you, Dr. Pike?"

The professor started fiddling with her bag. I could tell she was thinking about what not to tell me. Maybe my intuition was growing in Tiwa.

"I know that it was one of the properties formerly owned by Raymond Yardley. That's about it."

I couldn't shake the feeling she had chosen not to tell me everything.

"My mother got sick as soon as we moved into the building. Strange things have been happening to me. I don't know what to do. We just got here." My voice was growing stronger. I exhaled with relief at speaking my truth. I hoped that Dr. Pike would tell me what I needed to know. I also kind of hoped that she wouldn't.

"I'm sorry to hear about your mother," Dr. Pike said. She finally stopped messing with her bag and looked directly at me.

"Do you know anything? Do you know anything about Yardley Place? I can't find any information," I asked her.

"I-," Dr. Pike started then stopped. "Your mother. Do you know when she'll be able to come home? How is she?" Something told me that Dr. Pike was holding back an awful, ugly truth. I wasn't sure I wanted to know but I had to find out. But the fact that she was hiding it was infuriating.

I stood erect. Anger shot from my eyes. Why did she keep avoiding the subject? Why didn't she want to help? What was going on?

Teddy chimed in from the doorway. "I should have told you when you told me where you lived," he said, walking closer to us.

Dr. Pike and I turned to face him. She glared a warning of caution at him. I took a loud deep breath and waited. I looked back and forth between the two, hoping one of them would decide. Dr. Pike nodded, permitting Teddy to continue.

"There are so many stories about that house because it was owned by the Yardleys. It is where the Yardleys used to live. I should have told you when you told me about your mother getting sick." Now, Teddy found the floor interesting.

"When my mother got sick? What does that have to do with the building?" I demanded.

Dr. Pike finally decided to be forthcoming. "Raymond Yardley used to live there. With his family. He was known as an odd man. Malicious. He'd use his magic to play horrible games on people. He had so much money and power here, no one tried to stop him. Some time after he disappeared, his home was converted into apartments. I have heard stories of people experiencing strange things while living there. Your mother is not the first to get sick shortly after moving in. Lots of strange things have happened since Raymond Yardley disappeared decades ago."

"When you noticed the house at the museum, I should have told you then. Maybe I downplayed it. All the stories I'd heard," Teddy chimed in. "I didn't want to scare you."

My body tensed up. "Maybe you downplayed it?!" My fists shot to my side, my fingernails creating half-moon dents into my palms. Raised in the southside of Chicago, I could not contain myself. My feelings could not be controlled.

"I woke up the other night in the basement after being walked around like a rag doll around the building!" I shouted. I started counting on my fingers. "My mother is sick, the Helper Clinic didn't want to help, I'm seeing strange versions of me hopping out my bathroom mirror and illusions in the basement." I shifted my shoulder bag to the other side. I held myself on the podium to keep my hands to myself. "These are things that you tell people. You don't downplay them."

The last of my words echoed briefly throughout the classroom. Teddy's eyes bulged at my outburst before he hung his head. Dr. Pike clasped her bag close to her chest, her mouth agape. I closed my eyes and inhaled deeply. I couldn't believe I had yelled at them. This wasn't like me. Silence dripped around us like honey, viscous and sloppy.

"I don't know what's happening." My voice was soft. I opened my eyes and stared past them. "I wasn't in control of my body. I was walked all over that building against my will." I shuddered and met Teddy's eyes. "I don't know what to do," I pleaded.

Teddy raised both of his shoulders. "I don't know. I mean, I don't know anyone personally that's lived in the building. But when your mom got sick, it sounded like some of the other stories I heard."

I didn't know what to say. What could I do? I didn't really know anyone in Tiwa. The ones I did know were hiding things from me. Mom was at the Helper Clinic and couldn't help. How would I get through this?

"Hey." Teddy leaned forward and touched my hand resting on the podium.

"Don't touch me," I said, drawing my hand back quickly and slightly banging it on the wood. I immediately wanted to apologize but said nothing as I rubbed my fist.

"Sorry," Teddy continued, leaning away from me, the look of confusion fleeting upon his face. He stuttered slightly. "I...I can come stay with you and we can check out your apartment together. I can't imagine what this is like for you, being in a new place and dealing with all this. Alone." He leaned in close to me. I could sense he was being careful not to touch me this time. I could sense his sincerity. "I don't think there's anything that can harm you. It's just...creepy. Creepier than usual for Tiwa even," he finished.

I pondered the offer. I knew I needed help. I turned to Dr. Pike.

Dr. Pike shook her head. She grabbed her trembling hand to stop it. "I'm sorry, angel. I can't stay. I have to be with my family. I agree with Teddy though. I don't think you are in any danger. I do believe things will die down."

Was Dr. Pike scared of the building too? If even she wouldn't go near it, how could I continue to do this alone? I considered Teddy's offer a bit longer, my heart racing at the thought of being alone with him. He shifted his body away from me, giving me the space to think. Dr. Pike pulled her bag closer to her body, preparing to leave.

"Ok, Teddy. Will you come and stay with me to check out the building...and bring Loreen with you. If she can't come, then I'll do this alone." I turned and left the room before anyone could say anything else. I didn't feel better but nothing could make me feel worse than I did right now.

20

"Explain that to me again?" Loreen held a small clear cage with a lavender lid. Her overnight bag hung in the crook of her elbow in the opposite hand. She tilted her head to look up at Teddy.

Teddy shifted the weight of the backpack that hung on one shoulder, switched Adu's leash to the other hand, and nodded politely to the woman that walked past them. He looked back to make sure the woman was out of earshot before continuing.

"She said she woke up in the basement. Like her body was being treated like a doll and she couldn't move while she was being 'walked,'" he said, using the air quote gesture with his free hand, "and after she was given a tour of the building, she found herself alone in the basement."

Loreen watched the path ahead for a moment. "Possession?" she said under her breath.

Teddy heard her but didn't say anything. Possession was possible in Tiwa. Unless it was in ritual with spirits, it was rare. He didn't know much about people using it on others. He surveyed the walkway ahead.

Loreen inhaled sharply. "Do you like her, Teddy?"

"What?" He turned to see her looking away from him. She didn't look up or repeat the question. Adu's head was slightly turned to the side as she sauntered ahead, as if she was waiting for an answer as well.

"She's interesting...I think she's interesting," Teddy responded. He pulled his free arm behind his head and looked up in the sky.

"She's interesting because she's from the mainland?" Loreen's voice was curious yet held an undertone Teddy was familiar with. Her own badly disguised romantic interest in him was often exposed involuntarily. Although she'd become less reticent with her feelings, Teddy hadn't directly acknowledged them. He valued their friendship and didn't know how she'd react if he ever directly turned her down.

He let the moments pass as they drew nearer to Imani's home. The three-story building loomed ahead of them. He usually tried to ignore the building whenever he was near it or had to pass it. Yet each time, the windows seemed to watch over him and everything else in its purveyance. Almost as if it sat on a hill, Yardley Place seemed to stretch taller than all the other buildings, ensuring its grand nature was respected.

"It's just a building," Teddy said to himself in an attempt to prepare himself for the night ahead.

"I think she's been through something," Loreen interrupted Teddy's wary preparations. She was looking up, directly at him this time, her eyes squinting at the lowering sun.

"You mean the move? Or not knowing she was from Tiwa?" Teddy said, making eye contact.

"No. I mean something traumatic." Loreen stopped walking. She grabbed Teddy's wrist, prompting him to stop with her. Adu heeled at his side. The dog lay down, unbothered by the break.

Teddy returned a wave at a man walking across the street before facing Loreen.

She cleared her throat and smiled softly. "Just go slow...if you like her," she went on. "I know I've been undecided about a major, but I've been very focused in my psychology class. I might pursue that."

"Ok?"

"Some of the things she does are textbook for someone who's experienced trauma...maybe even a type of assault." Loreen maintained eye contact.

Teddy understood that she was coming from a place of concern, not jealousy. He looked ahead and remembered Imani drawing her hand back when he had touched it earlier in the day. He thought about her always inviting Loreen to join them. Even after Loreen expressed obvious contempt for her. Teddy felt guilt gnaw at him from the inside out. He'd completely missed all the signs. Guilt transformed into sadness when he considered all of the horrible possibilities that Imani could have endured. Resolve grew. He needed to help her with whatever was going on in the building. And he needed to put his feelings aside to do it.

Teddy met Loreen's imploring gaze. "So, you like her then? You want to be her friend?" he joked. Loreen rolled her eyes, huffed, and walked ahead.

"Whatever, Teddy," she called back.

2 1

I sat cross-legged on my bed, not too far from Loreen. She sat on the edge of the bed, ready to run at any unnatural sight or sound. Teddy sat in the rolling chair at the desk, swaying in it from side to side, his long legs serving as an anchor.

"I appreciate you guys coming over," I said. My face was languid as I searched the bedroom for my next words. "This is the only room I've felt safe in. The only room where nothing has happened." I eyed the design on my comforter.

Loreen scooted further back towards the headboard. "Well, the salt at the front door and bedroom door will be helpful. We should be good for now."

"And we have Adu!" Teddy referred to his dog who was keeping watch in the living room. Soft paws could be heard padding down the hallway at the mention of its name. "Not now, Adu," Teddy called out. The paws sounded back down the hallway towards the living room.

I smiled at Teddy then caught Loreen's expression. Was it concern? Was Loreen a little scared herself? Loreen averted my gaze and got up to examine her tiny gecko in its cage on the nightstand.

"I don't think you ever told me your familiar's name, Loreen?"

"Iranran. His name is Iranran," Loreen responded. Her tone lacked her usual condescension.

"Oh!" I jumped up and walked in Teddy's direction. His head perked up as if he was waiting for directions.

I reached for the laptop sitting on the desk behind him. "I want my friend, Keisha, to help," I said and called my friend on video chat.

Introductions were made. Keisha and I exchanged knowing looks after I put the camera on Loreen and Teddy. With Keisha and my new friends in the same room, I felt a warmth I'd missed since arriving in Ibeji Village. I was ready to begin.

"I tried to do some research after I started experiencing things," I started. I placed the laptop next to Teddy and returned to the bed. Each time I wanted to look at Keisha, I could see him, too. His face was comforting. Loreen maintained her spot on the bed next to me. She was probably keeping the same view as me.

"I'm not even sure if I truly saw what I saw. Like the time my reflection didn't move the same way I did. Or, when I was in the basement and I saw a woman chasing me as a little girl." I went on, describing the strange things I'd seen, including Mom's contorted shape, the reaction of the Helper Clinic, the evil looking reflection of me, and being walked around like a puppet only to awaken in the basement. I glanced around. Everyone had a fearful look on their face, but it was more pronounced on those actually in the room. Silence held us all captive for a moment.

"How could you see yourself as a child in the building?" Loreen asked disdainfully. "I thought you weren't in Tiwa at that age? I thought you didn't remember?"

"I don't know. I know I wasn't in Tiwa at that time, so I couldn't have been in the building. And I don't know who that woman was. But that little girl, she looked just like me. Skin color, facial features, and smile." I shook my head. "I don't know. I remember that smell when I saw the vision. It hit me hard. That's why I wanted the morning glory when we went to the magic shop. That's what I think I smelled."

The room was quiet as everyone took in what I had shared with them.

"That's not much to go on," Teddy finally said. "We should do more research. All this time I've only heard stories, but never anything about what causes the hauntings. Let's look into that."

"What's the name of the building again?" Keisha called out from the laptop.

"Yardley Place," I called out, "previously owned by Raymond Yardley."

"His wife was Elizabeth Yardley," Loreen called out.

"Didn't they have a daughter?" Teddy asked. He pulled out his phone. "You look up the daughter, I'll look up the building. Imani and Keisha, you take Raymond and his wife," Teddy directed.

Keisha and I exchanged smirks before heading to our phones to start the research.

Murmurs of frustration and deep heavy sighs filled the room moments later. We came to a consensus on how difficult it was to find anything other than information about Raymond Yardley. "I can't even find a picture of his daughter," Loreen exclaimed.

"I can't find a picture of his wife," Keisha added.

"I found this picture...of him and the house staff. Maybe they're in it," Teddy advised, holding the phone up for Loreen and me to look at more closely.

Loreen grabbed the phone and zoomed in on all the people, moving around the picture to look at their faces.

"Wait," I interrupted. "That's Raymond. Who's that little boy next to him?"

The three of us huddled in closer to look at the boy. His tiny face was nearly covered by his large afro. He had a sweet smile and stood posed with his hands behind his back, like the other staff. Teddy took the phone back from Loreen and zoomed out.

"It only has the first name of the kid. It says his name is Gabriel," Teddy said.

"Wait," Keisha called out from the laptop. "I thought Raymond had a daughter." The three of us turned to face Keisha. Disappointment filled the room. I moved away from Teddy and Loreen towards the head of the bed, my shoulders dropping with my head. "How are we going to find anything if there is nothing to find?" I cried out softly.

"Girl, we'll figure it out," Keisha said from inside the laptop. "I'll even do what I can from here on the mainland."

"That's why you're my girl," I said, walking over and picking up the laptop from my desk. I sat back on the bed to continue the conversation. "I miss you, lady. I miss the mainland."

Keisha smiled. "I miss you, too. I know this has been hard, moving there and dealing with all this crazy stuff. Bright side though, I bet it's a distraction from Rome."

My heart sank at the mention of the name. I glanced up to see if Teddy and Loreen had heard her. Loreen gave a slight nod to Teddy when she caught his eye. Teddy shook his head, appearing to rebuke her.

Rage flared from behind my eyes when I looked back at Keisha. "Don't say his name," I seethed from behind closed teeth.

"I'm so sorry, Imani," Keisha started. "I just meant, this move...and all this stuff..." her voice trailed off. "How's your mom doing?" she started again, changing the subject.

I pulled myself together after a little time and noticed Teddy and Loreen shift around in their seats. "She's better," I answered. "I'm going to visit her in the morning. She can have visitors." I didn't mention that she'd been able to have visitors for a couple days. I just hadn't made it.

"Tell her I said hi. Give her my love," Keisha said before waving goodbye and ending the call.

22

"Who's hungry?" Imani asked the other two as she headed out the bedroom door to the kitchen. Teddy and Loreen both replied, "I could eat," in unison, sending the trio into a fit of laughter.

She searched the kitchen for something quick and acceptable to give to her guests. What was the staple dinner one served guests in Tiwa? She decided she would need to research that later. An idea lingered like a snake waiting for its prey that her body could be taken over at any moment. Whatever she was going to make would have to be quick and fulfilling. She identified some red beans and rice she could throw together and began gathering the ingredients and cookware.

"What about Adu?" Imani called down the long dark hall. "What does she-"

The glass measuring cup dropped from Imani's hands. Her body tensed up; her mind went blank. She withdrew into a trance-like state. The shattering glass echoed throughout the apartment. Adu, Teddy, and Loreen ran into the kitchen.

"Imani?" Teddy gasped when he saw her. Her eyes were rolled so far in the back of her head that only the sclera could be seen. Her body hung in suspended animation, arms at her sides, palms spread, her feet a few inches from the ground.

Loreen released a bloodcurdling scream. The hair on Adu's back was raised as she backed out of the kitchen.

"You are back. I have you now," the voice of a man sounded from Imani's moving lips. Teddy slowly approached his floating friend, unsure of what to do next. He couldn't hear Loreen's soft cries calling out Imani's name. A sharp bark from Adu brought them both back to the moment.

"We have to help her, Loreen. What do we do?" Teddy and Loreen shared a frightened look. Loreen's face brightened when an idea came to her. A plan.

"I'll be right back. Keep an eye on her."

Loreen returned with a box of small candles, opening them to pull out two white ones. "Here, take these," she commanded while lighting the candles and handing them to Teddy. Teddy did as he was told and waited for her instructions. Loreen scoured the kitchen cabinets until she found a clear white bowl and the salt. She cleaned the bowl with salt and water, praying as she did so.

"You are back, I have you now," the man's voice sounded again. Visibly scared, Loreen placed the water in the space below Imani's floating feet, using caution so not to touch her. She took the candles from Teddy, spilled some hot wax on the tile floor on either side of Imani and stuck the candles to the floor.

Teddy went back and forth from observing Loreen in action to examining Imani in my possessed state. "What else can I do?" he asked, his voice trembling with fear.

"You are back, I have you now," the voice repeated.

"Be ready, Teddy," Loreen started. "We're going to use a spell my grandmother taught me. If it works, you'll have to catch her before she hits the ground and we'll rush back to the room."

Teddy nodded. "I'm ready."

Loreen grabbed a bottle of brandy from her search of the cabinets, took the cap off, and grabbed the tub of salt in the same hand. She started a rhythmic clap, using her hand against her knee. Teddy joined the rhythm with his hands. Loreen began dancing in a circle around Imani, careful to avoid the candles. With a measured flair, she sprinkled salt in a circle, keeping the candles on the outside. Teddy joined the dance, helping Loreen keep the rhythm.

"You are back, I have you now."

Loreen and Teddy danced in a circle while Loreen chanted to the beat: "We pray that you release Imani. We ask that you let her go. We pray that you release Imani. We ask that you let her go. We pray that you release Imani. We ask that you let her go."

Upon her final recitation, Loreen took a swig of the brandy into her cheeks and spit it at Imani's suspended body. The flame from the candles flickered then grew large. Adu growled from her post just outside the kitchen. The flames went out. The voice coming from Imani stopped. Her eyes returned to their normal state. She fell towards the ground, into Teddy's waiting arms.

He carried Imani into her room where Loreen added more salt to the doorway. He placed her gently on the bed and pulled the desk chair over to her bedside. Loreen ignored the tinges of jealousy she felt in her chest as she watched Teddy watching over Imani. She knew Imani would be okay but wondered if Teddy understood that as well.

"She'll be okay, Teddy."

"I know," he said, not daring to move his gaze. The tenderness he displayed reminded Loreen why she had fallen for him all those years ago. Teddy was a good guy. He would help anyone who needed it and all of Ibeji Village knew that. Why couldn't she understand that the help he was giving Imani was different?

* * *

"What happened?" I sat up in the bed. Loreen looked at me as if she was impressed. I wondered what I'd done to earn the look.

"Woah, woah. Don't move too fast," Teddy said with a laugh in his voice.

"I'm okay. I'm good," I replied. "I thought I was in the kitchen making some red beans and rice."

"Well, you definitely made a mess," Teddy joked.

Loreen and Teddy explained what they had seen. Teddy described how Loreen jumped into action. "I think I was so worried, I froze," he added.

"Aw, you were worried about me?" I smiled. Loreen watched as I let the smile go quickly. As if she could sense that I didn't feel comfortable getting too comfortable. "I'm glad you two were here," I finished, flatly.

"I'll take the floor," Teddy announced as he started spreading a small unfilled air mattress between the desk and the floor. Loreen reached into her bag and pulled out sleeping clothes.

"You two are spending the night?" I couldn't hide the surprise and joy I felt from my voice.

"Of course. After what we just witnessed, there's no way we're leaving you alone tonight," Teddy said. His voice was still shaky. Loreen seemed to be watching him too. As if she could tell he was hiding something. She rolled her eyes and grabbed her clothes, a small bag, and her gecko's cage.

"I'm going to change in the bathroom. I'll be right back," she called out.

"Um..." I started.

"Don't worry. I'll be fine. I'll be right back." She closed the bedroom door behind her, smiling back. I couldn't not return the smile.

"I don't know what to say. I am so glad you two are staying, even after what you witnessed. Thank you," I said. Teddy was using an electronic pump to blow up his bed as I grabbed a large blanket out of her wardrobe. Was he avoiding eye contact? I imagined him seeing me like that was like when I had found her mom hovering above my bed. He was probably still processing it. "You came very prepared," I continued, changing the subject as I handed him the blanket.

"You can never be too prepared. If you stay ready, you don't have to get ready." He winked at me. "Thanks."

He seemed to be okay. Loreen came back into the room unscathed, wearing a long lavender sleeping gown with a matching robe.

"You sure have gotten fancy since your cartoon bear onesies," Teddy teased. Yeah, he was okay.

"Hush," Loreen hissed.

Neither Loreen nor I tried to hide as we watched Teddy remove his shirt and pants. He stood in long loose boxers. "Ladies," he exclaimed in fake shock, clutching his chest. We all giggled and headed into our beds,

Loreen sharing the bed with me while Teddy was on his air mattress that was a few inches too short for him.

"Does anyone need anything? I didn't even feed y'all," I said.

"No!" Teddy and Loreen yelled in unison. We all let out a nervous laugh.

"Loreen?" I said before hitting the light switch.

"Mmhm?" Loreen responded from under the covers. She was facing the wall.

"Thank you."

Loreen turned over and gave me a smile. Then she rolled back over towards the wall. "Girl, go to sleep," she said, humor playing in her voice.

"OK, goodnight. Thanks again." I returned the smile to the back of Loreen's head.

23

Tuesday

The rest of the night was uneventful in the apartment. I slept well for one of the first times in the apartment, dreaming of walking around Ibeji Village with a red cardinal on my shoulder. Sharing the bed with Loreen felt like the sleepovers I used to have with Keisha, minus the possession. I wasn't even bothered by Teddy's presence in the room. I knew having Loreen there helped with that. And also knowing that he would help me when I needed it made it more comfortable.

In the morning, each of us had our mission to complete. "I'm going to try to talk to some people to find more information." Teddy stood by the front door and put his backpack over his shoulder. I was amazed he was able to deflate, fold, and fit the air mattress into the confines of the backpack. Adu waited off leash for his command.

"I'll do some more research online and see if I can find anything," Loreen said, gathering her things. She gave me a one-sided hug. "Call us if you need anything."

I hugged her back and opened the front door for them. "Thanks for your help. I appreciate it. I'll talk to you after I visit my mom," I said before closing the door behind them.

* * *

"You look good...but tired. How are you? I like your hair." Mom reached out and grabbed one of my loose long braids which served as a sort of bang. The rest had been twisted into a crown-style around my head. I bent down, kissed her cheek, then gently pulled the hair back behind my ear when I sat in the chair next to her bed. The sound of the TV in the room dulled to the background.

"I'm okay," I drew out. "How are you?" I leaned in closer to her, wanting to lay my head on her but pulling back to avoid causing any injury.

Mom wrapped her arms around my head and pulled it down to rest on her chest. She inhaled deeply and began rubbing my back. "I missed you, baby."

I leaned into the hug and relaxed on her chest. Her gown smelled sanitized; nothing like her. But I still felt comforted by the touch of her hand circling my back.

"When are you coming home, Mom?" I peeked an eye up at her, catching her chin pointed up and her eyes staring at the ceiling. I enjoyed the movement of my head going up and down slowly with each of her inhales and exhales.

"Soon, I think. I hope," she said. "The Helpers here haven't been able to figure out what happened, but they've been pretty good at managing the symptoms. They want to be sure the same thing doesn't happen again when I go home."

I traced the curlicues on Mom's gown. "So, they don't know what happened? Why you were contorted and catatonic?" I felt her heartbeat speed up a bit. Maybe the Helpers didn't tell her how she had been found. I didn't think they believed me anyway. They would have if they'd been in the apartment last night.

"No. They don't." She didn't ask for any more information. I assumed that she either didn't know or didn't want to know. I decided not to share about my own temporary catatonia.

We embraced each other for a moment longer before I sat up. I looked around the room, realizing this was my first time in a Helper Clinic. A place I'd only read about.

"This is nice for a hospital," I said, taking in the large private room. The small couch in the room was plush and could fit two, maybe even three people. The television sat high on the wall, similar to hospital rooms on the mainland. The large wooden door didn't have a window in it, making the room more private. "It's like an actual bedroom. It doesn't feel like a hospital."

Mom nodded. "A lot of work goes into making patients feel like they're at home. It helps with speed and quality of recovery."

I looked back at her with my eyes squinting and mouth turned up. "You sure know a lot. Why didn't you tell me any of this?"

An air of expectation hung around us like a heavy, thick fog. I knew she knew what I was asking.

"What have you been doing? Have you had a chance to unpack?" Mom said, fixing the blanket around her.

I watched her hands gliding across the bed, smoothing out the non-existent wrinkles.

"Almost done. Oh yeah, Keisha says hi and hopes you're feeling better," I said.

"I'm glad you've reached out to her since we got here," she said. How many wrinkles did she see in the bed?

"Mmhm. I've made a couple of friends from one of my classes and Keisha has been helping us work on a class project about one of the prominent families in Ibeji Village, The Yardleys."

Mom looked up from the bed at the mention of the name. Her face turned stoic and her body became unnaturally still. I waited for her to say something. She neither moved nor spoke.

"Are you ok, Mom? Do you need anything?"

She winced. "Just my stomach. I'm fine. Have you been meditating?" She drew her shoulders in and studied her clasped hands. "Remember, it will help you increase your focus. And it's important that you're following the traditions of Ibeji Village to help with your magic."

I slunk down in the chair and frowned. "No. It's all been a lot with you gone."

She nodded, lifting her head slightly. "I get it. But you can at least start with honoring your ancestors and starting to build your relationship with them through an altar. It'd be easy to build."

I sat straight up in the chair, my jaw tight. "Mom. How can I talk to my ancestors if I don't know who they are?" My nostrils flared. "Why didn't you tell me we were from Tiwa all this time? I don't get it."

Mom cleared her throat. "I..." she stammered. "It's all complicated." She shook her head. "I just wasn't close to my family when I left."

I leaned in.

A pained expression crossed her face. "I love Tiwa and I've missed it all these years. I still practiced and maintained the rituals in the mainland. I knew I'd come back one day."

Memories of Mom's chanting and her upkeep with altars sprang up from my memory. I remembered some of the times when she'd try to teach me about the rituals, but I hadn't been interested at that time. She eventually gave up.

"Praying daily and communicating with your ancestors will help with some of the stress you have in your life," Mom had implored after my situation with Rome. "Leaving offerings for them would be even better." I had still ignored it, even then. Praying did not seem like the solution that would help me through my trauma. Here she was again, recommending the same thing. Maybe there was something there.

"When your father gave me the gift of you," Mom continued, "I let go of the idea of returning to Tiwa and focused on raising you. I didn't know when I'd be able to return."

I sat quietly at the mention of my father. I realized I could count on one hand the number of times she had mentioned him. And each time, I was unprepared to ask anything else about him.

"I wish you'd told me something," I mumbled. "Anything."

Mom looked back to the floral pattern on the blanket. She placed her hand on her stomach and looked back at me. "Could you call a Helper on your way out? I'm not feeling well. Come back tomorrow. We'll talk more."

24

I fingered the photos of strangers that sat on Mom's altar. The water in the glass bowl on the altar was cloudy and the flower was now only a droopy brown stem with withered petals. I tingled with shame as I thought about how careless I had been in taking care of Mom's altar during her absence. A quick glide of the peacock feather across my fingertips and I decided to rectify the situation.

I washed out the glass bowl with salt, the way I'd seen Mom do in the past. Focused on the intention of connecting with my ancestors, I scrubbed the glass and rinsed it off. *"Intention is important,"* Mom's voice rang out in my head. I dusted the altar and pictures, placing everything back the way she had it. My shame began to dissipate.

"Never blow out the candles. If you blow out the candle, you blow out your intention," her voice rang out in my head. I lit the white candle and incense. I shook the incense flame out and placed the stick on the altar. The scent was floral, jasmine, and reminded me of Mom. I sat on the floor in front of the altar and inhaled. Entranced by the smell, I closed my eyes and focused on my breathing.

Blackness and breath gave me solace. I allowed my stomach to grow large with inhales and deflate with long exhales. Soon, I was focused only on the blackness. *"Ground yourself to the Earth,"* Mom had taught me. I imagined a large root extending from my seated bottom into the Earth. A calmness came over me as the imaginary root dug into the ground.

"Imagine a place that is home for you. See yourself going there." I

envisioned myself draped in purple, floating above the ocean under the glow of the full moon. I traveled miles, letting the waves crash below me and feeling droplets from the spray on the exposed parts of my body. My hand scraped the water's surface before I landed softly on white sand. Ahead of me stood a modern cabin filled with large glass windows. My place of peace. I imagined heading to the cabin and entering, leaving gifts at the entrance for the spirits that protected it.

"Now pray."

I saw myself in the cabin, looking out into the moonlit ocean. The waves lapped gently at the shore. In my mind's eye, I thanked my ancestors for my health, Mom, and the safe journey to Tiwa and Ibeji Village. I asked for strength to heal and to face whatever was going on in the building. In the midst of asking for Mom to have strength, the ocean began to disappear from me. I tried to focus and imagine more detail in the cabin.

Instead, I saw Yardley Place in front of me, as it used to be. Before it was renovated into apartments. I tried to break from the vision but found myself unable to move. I was no longer in control of my meditation. Panic rose in my chest, but I couldn't move. I was now looking at myself and a young man I'd never met. We sat in a bedroom I'd never seen.

25

The girl sits on the bed, close to the boy, their legs pressing against each other. She holds his hand in her lap and rests her head on his shoulder, her long braids draping down over his Helper uniform. "Thank you for being there for me. I couldn't have done this without you," she says sweetly. His face lights up. He fights the urge to look at her, distracting himself with the wall.

"We have to keep him tied up," she continues. She lifts her head off his shoulder and pulls his chin to face her. "But I have a plan for how we can make some money to get out of here."

The boy nods, encouraging her to continue. He stares deeply into her eyes, entranced by each word that leaves her lips.

"With all the Helpers gone, all we have to do now is keep the businesses running as long as possible." She begins stroking his arm and his smile gets impossibly bigger. "I'll be his assistant and head off as many phone calls and decisions as possible. Luckily, he was already working here and not leaving Tiwa as often for his business on the mainland. We don't have to actually meet with anyone, but..." Her voice trails off. She reaches up and pulls his head down to her. She looks into his eyes and kisses him softly on the lips. He meets her lips and holds the kiss a second longer than she expects. Their eyes twinkle when they meet. She squeezes his hand.

"Do you think you could imitate him? If you had to speak to someone on the phone as though you were him?" She waits patiently as he thinks about it.

"Get out," he says, matching the same tone and voice that she heard a few years back from her father. She flinches but maintains a smile, her grasp within his, and nods approvingly.

"That works. Once we have enough of the money, we can leave Tiwa."

He speaks with his own voice. "Leave Tiwa? I thought we'd just leave Ibeji Village. Not leave Tiwa. I still have my mother and my-"

She kisses him to silence him. He embraces her. "We don't have to leave Tiwa. There are so many other places in Tiwa we can be," she says reassuringly.

He smiles and initiates the kiss this time.

* * *

I opened my eyes and saw the altar and Mom's belongings around me. I was back in the apartment. I was released from the vision.

"How could that be me? How is it possible?" I said aloud, rising slowly from the floor. My head felt clear and refreshed but I still felt somewhat unstable after the vision. A little out of control. A million thoughts ran through my head, trying to make sense of how I could have lived in Tiwa as a teenager and not remember anything. How I could know and interact with other people I didn't remember, like the boy. The boy.

My steps were light but I hurried down the hallway and into my bedroom. The afternoon light shined on my laptop on the desk. I went through the saved pictures I had for the building and the Yardleys and found the staff picture Teddy had found before.

"He's there," I said to no one. My finger pointed to the boy standing next to Raymond Yardley, his afro nearly bigger than his face. He looked just like the boy in my vision. Instead, in this picture, he was much younger but still dressed as staff.

26

Wednesday

I couldn't remember ever being this turned off and bored by Tiwa history. Yet, here I was, feet tapping and body waiting until Dr. Pike finished and excused the other section of her History of Tiwa class. I pushed past all the students filing out of the class to get in and meet Dr. Pike at the front. Teddy and Loreen joined us right after- per the directive I texted them. Teddy looked confused, Loreen's face sustained disdain, and Dr. Pike was ready to help.

"I had another vision last night," I began, opening up my laptop. "It looked like me again, but I don't remember it ever happening." I pulled up the picture of Raymond Yardley and his staff. "This boy was in the vision." I pointed to the child with the large afro. "But he was older. And we knew each other well. We kissed."

I saw Loreen eye Teddy. He was scrunching up his face when I mentioned the kiss. Did he like me? Did she know? If he knew how uncomfortable it was for me to see the kiss, he probably wouldn't have his face fixed like that. Confusion outweighed my discomfort. I couldn't process actually kissing a boy. Seeing the couple's affection for each other nearly sent my head spinning.

"Do any of you know who this might be?" I asked, tapping where the boy with the big hair stood. I needed to keep the focus off the kiss.

Teddy and Loreen shook their heads "no." Dr. Pike squinted at the picture, scrutinizing it further. "Well, he's definitely staff in the house, by the way he's dressed. Traditionally, in Tiwa, the staff is delineated by certain patterns and colors. In the Village of Iku, house staff generally wear a type of animal print in the form of a sash or belt. However, depending on the seniority of the staff, the location, and type of fabric worn..."

"Thank you, Dr. Pike," I cut the professor off. "So, Raymond Yardley hired a child as staff?"

"That's uncommon," Loreen chimed in.

"Yes," Dr. Pike said. "Perhaps, he was the child of someone on the staff. It is more usual, yet still not common, for a parent who is house staff to have their child live with them in the home."

I considered the information. "In my vision, the boy and I were talking about imitating someone, keeping them tied up, and taking their money."

"How did the vision start?" Teddy asked. "Was it like before when you were possessed?"

I shook my head. "I was practicing meditation and the vision just came to me."

Loreen sneered. "Oh, the mainlander is working on her magic."

I couldn't tell if she was praising or belittling me. I ignored the comment. Her behavior was really hard to read after the incident in the apartment. "Maybe the building is trying to tell me something about the disappearance of Raymond Yardley," I concluded.

"Why you?" Loreen was curt this time. Nice Loreen must've run out of time.

"I don't know. Like I said, I was in the vision, again. That has to mean something. Maybe it's not actually me, but a way to encourage me to help." Even on the fly, that sounded like a more valid reason for why I would be showing up in the visions. The rest of the group nodded absently.

"You should go to the Helper's Archive," Dr. Pike suggested.

"Yes! Why didn't we think of that earlier." Teddy was loud and excited, throwing his hands into the air. He looked at us and pulled his hands down to his side. "That would be a good place to start," he finished calmly.

"What is the Helper's Archive?" I closed my laptop and placed it in my bag.

"There you can get any public information they have about the case," Dr. Pike offered. She also started packing her belongings.

"It's kind of like the police station on the mainland," Loreen started. "Except there's more than just law enforcement. Also, they're more helpful and less dangerous." Her tone exhibited a warranted superciliousness.

"I'll go with you," Teddy chimed in. "I can show you where it's at."

"We can show you where it's at," Loreen volunteered.

"Don't you three have more classes?" Dr. Pike called out to us.

"Aw, c'mon, Dr. Pike." Teddy looked back with his most charming smile. "We have to help Imani."

I couldn't help but giggle.

* * *

The windows outside the Helper's Archive building were mirror plated. They reflected and shone the color of the sky and clouds that passed by it. A red bird appeared to be coupled up as it flew past the building. I covered my eyes to block out the glare while I stopped to take in the number of windows that surrounded the building. The design of the building was awe inspiring. I noticed how the circular walls appeared to wrap around themselves and, with the design of the windows, the building was nearly invisible from the outside. It was only the large lettering of the "Helper's Archive" sign and the sliding of the giant nonreflective glass doors that allowed the building to be seen.

"You should see the inside," Teddy said, breaking the spell the building had on me.

We walked through the automatic sliding doors. A Helper sat behind a desk labeled "INFORMATION", smiling at us as we approached.

"Ba wo ni? Welcome to the Helper's Archive," the woman began in a singsong voice. Her curly bob danced along with her words. "What is the purpose of your visit today?" It kind of reminded me of some of the other times I had visited an information desk in Chicago, like at the police station. But, no one had been helpful when I had gone to the police station a couple of years ago. At best, they were condescending and unable to listen to me as I recounted my trauma. The energy I felt from this woman was different. Her words were scripted but they still sounded genuine.

"Ba wo. We need help for a school project," Loreen responded. "We're studying the history of Ibeji Village and doing a report on the disappearance of Raymond Yardley." The helper's face changed into a mix of pity and empathy.

"So sad," she said, placing her hand to her heart. "I just can't believe that he hasn't been found all this time. Well, nobody knows the mysteries that lie at the bottom of the ocean." The Helper pulled out a small map of the layout of the building. "Have you ever visited the Helper's Archive before?" A small smile crossed her face.

We all shook our heads. "Well, you're in for a treat!" she said. I started to doubt her authenticity as the smile on her face grew more with her excitement.

"Here at the Helper's Archive, we have several departments to support the community," the Helper continued. "Investigators, Interpreters, Advocates, Counselors, and Resources. For your project, you will go to the Investigators department, here." She highlighted the path to the Investigator Department and circled its location with a purple pen. "If you need any more assistance, there is an information desk on each floor of the Helper's Archive."

I was confused by how the woman read. Her professional voice was skewing the perception of her sincere desire to help. If it was sincere. I searched Teddy and Loreen's faces for any similar confusion as they headed to the escalator. They were focused on heading to the Investigator Department. My lack of discernment must've been part of the cultural differences between Tiwans and mainlanders.

"The Investigators are like detectives," Loreen said, misunderstanding my confused look. I gave a quick nod as we headed to the Investigator's department.

I couldn't help but wonder who did the cleaning in the building. The escalator sides, handrails, and steps were made of clear glass. The hallways were covered with opaque glass, separating the different departments, that would still require just as much cleaning as the escalator. I waited for a Helper with cleaning supplies to pop out and clean behind us as we touched the glass on the handrail, our footsteps as we traveled down the hallway, and our fingers as we touched the glass door entrance of the Investigator Department. No one came.

The Helper at the information desk inside the Investigator Department was equally helpful and pleasant as her counterpart at the entrance to the building. I watched the tilt of her head and listened to her sing-song voice as she provided directions to Public Information. *Maybe they just really love what they do,* I thought to myself.

"So we just wait until they call our number. Then we get to meet with an investigator," Teddy reiterated as we sat in the waiting room.

I sat in the large black armchairs across from Teddy and Loreen. I needed space to take everything in but wasn't given much time. The investigator called our number quickly and led us to the back. Similar to the rest of the building, the office he led us to was surrounded by opaque glass walls. The doors slid closed on their own, as smoothly and quietly as when they had opened. The investigator motioned for us to sit across from him at the small table.

"Ba wo ni? Here is the public file for Raymond Yardley's disappearance. Do you have any questions?" The investigator was short in height and patience. His brown bald head was just as shiny as the rest of the building. I searched the room for a Helper that would come out and shine his head. No one came.

Teddy looked through the file, either unaware or not caring about the investigator's impatience. He passed each piece to Loreen and me after he studied them. "This says that the house staff was investigated after the disappearance of Raymond and his daughter, Reyna Yardley,"

Teddy pointed out. Loreen and I leaned in closer to look at the document he was referring to.

"It does," the investigator replied dryly.

"Reyna was her name? She disappeared too? I never knew any of that." Loreen met my look. We both seemed shocked about the information.

"It's public knowledge." The investigator stared at us as if his look would make us move faster.

"I didn't know either, Loreen," Teddy said softly. "Can we see the staff interviews?" Teddy was curt with the investigator. "Specifically, any children of the staff?"

The light bounced off six different places on the investigator's head as he shook it. "Any interviews of those under eighteen are not made available to the public. Their names are held from any public files."

"I don't see any pictures of Reyna," I noted, flipping through some of the pages again.

"She was a minor at the time of her disappearance." The investigator's tone remained unchanged regardless of who spoke to him. I watched and saw his patience physically fizzle, like a candle that was blown out. "This copy of the public file is for you to keep. Now, unless you have any further questions..." The investigator stood and motioned towards the door.

"We don't," Loreen advised and stood. Teddy and I joined her. "Eshe," Loreen said, walking with us out the door.

27

"Tell Keisha we said hi!" Teddy hollered. I stepped out of my bedroom, closed the door, and headed down the hallway to the living room to take the video call privately. I thought it would have been nice if Adu had been here with us. I scanned the room quickly for anything out of sort, bounced on the couch, and returned to the call.

"Hey lady!" I grinned at my friend. Of course, Keisha's makeup was immaculate, especially next to my bare skin and puffy eyes on the screen.

"Was that Teddy I heard?" Keisha inquired playfully. She watched me carefully.

"Yea." My voice was more energetic than I looked. "He and Loreen are here. We just got back from the Helper's Archive. What are you all dolled up for?"

"Nowhere special. The Helper's Archive? What's that?"

I explained the visit and what we had learned so far about Raymond's disappearance, including his daughter, Reyna, and her disappearance at the same time. "We're going to go over the file more closely now."

"I wish I'd have read more about Tiwa now. I didn't understand how differently things operate there. There are some similarities too."

I thought about the investigator's demeanor and how it mirrored some of the experience I had when I had to deal with the police in Chicago. I thought maybe I wouldn't have given up my fight if I'd been received with more compassion in Chicago. I almost wondered how that situation would have been dealt with in Tiwa. If the Investigators would have given a young woman in my position compassion- and actual help.

"Right?" I said to Keisha. "Despite everything, it's nice that I get to see what I actually used to read about. I'm starting to learn more about the traditions and rituals. It feels surprisingly good to feel connected like this."

"How's your mom?"

"She's doing better."

"Did you find anything else out from her?"

I reflected on the questions Mom had avoided, the things she refused to address and figured that was something. "She only told me that she left when she was really young and that she's not very close to her family. That when she had me, she just focused on raising me." I shrugged.

Keisha nodded and returned the shrug. "That sounds like Ms. Brena. I remember how she used to be at all the fieldtrips when we were in elementary school," Keisha laughed.

"We couldn't get away with nothing," I added.

We laughed as we each pondered different memories during the times we were able to spend in person. I felt myself getting even more energized by the reminiscing.

"I know I can't do much from over here, but I'd like to stay on the call with you all. It's kind of like I'm there and hanging out."

I put the phone in front of my face and looked directly into Keisha's eyes. "Don't bring him up again." The firmness in my voice was chilling, even to me. We both knew I wasn't talking about Teddy. Keisha gave a single nod.

"Do you get the sense that Loreen likes Teddy?" She changed the subject. I embraced it.

"Yea. Probably." I fidgeted with the couch's piping.

"I think he likes you." If nothing, Keisha was always blunt.

"Yea. Maybe."

Keisha let silence hang between us. A laugh between Teddy and Loreen, muffled by the door, filled the living room.

"He seems like a good guy...and he's very handsome," I started. "But I really can't imagine trusting, let alone dating, a man right now. I don't think I'm ready." The couch had tiny grooves in its pattern.

"I don't know how long these things take but take as much time as you need. Two years for you is not the same as two years for another person."

"Mmhm."

"I wonder why he's not into Loreen, though."

"I was wondering that, too. We've been so focused on all this other stuff happening, I haven't really had a chance to get to know her better. She's getting more tolerable, but she's still not making it easier. Last night-"

A door down the hall was flung open. "We found something, Imani!" Teddy called out from the bedroom. I ran with the phone down the hall to join them.

Papers from the file were strewn across my bed. A few sheets had fallen on the floor. Teddy and Loreen stood hunched over the others on the desk.

"Excuse me." I reached between the pair and positioned the phone on the desk so that Keisha could at least see some of us while we talked. Loreen and Teddy moved out of the way without breaking their concentration. I joined them and stood to examine the contents of the file. "What are we looking at?"

"This is where you live." Teddy waved a hand at all the papers. All of them had pictures of different rooms and almost nothing looked like the home that I was in now. There were some similarities, though.

"This is before it was renovated to apartment buildings," Loreen added. "The investigators took pictures after Raymond and Reyna Yardley's disappearance. I don't know if it was necessity or curiosity, but they took a lot of pictures."

I scanned through the photos. The gaudiness of the furniture struck me as odd, but nothing gave a clue to what we were dealing with.

"The file says that Raymond's wife, Elizabeth, had already died several years before their disappearance," Loreen said.

"Did it say how she died?" I continued to examine the photos of the home individually.

"Heart failure," Teddy said matter-of-factly.

"That's sad. How old was Reyna when her mother died? How old was she when she disappeared?"

Loreen went to the bed and reached among the scattered paperwork. "It doesn't say how old she was when her mother died, but she was almost eighteen when she and her father disappeared."

"Hm." The picture in my hand distracted me. I was trying to place where I'd seen the bedding and decor. "My vision," I whispered out loud.

"What is it?" Keisha was looking intently through the screen at my face for signs of what I had realized.

"This is the room I was in during my vision. This is probably Reyna's room." Loreen and Teddy glanced at what I held in my hand. Loreen began searching for something among the photos. "Why would I be in the visions?" I asked.

"Sometimes visions work like that." Teddy shrugged.

"Sounds like a dream where you can be a different person," Keisha added.

"Yup, just like that," Teddy agreed.

"This is where the room is in the home. It's a picture of the layout." Loreen handed me a photo of a large closed wooden door, followed by another picture of the door opening to the same bedding, furniture and decor.

"You recognize something else, don't you?" Keisha saw the look on my face.

I smiled at her then looked back to the photo. "I do. I think this is the apartment I was placed in front of when I was possessed."

"Hmm," Teddy muttered.

"There aren't any pictures of Reyna or Elizabeth. Not even in the pictures on the walls of the house. Only Raymond." Loreen had shuffled through the pictures, moving them side to side. "Wait, here's the same picture of the staff that we saw online." Teddy and I leaned in to look at the picture.

"Seems like we're in the same place we started." I sighed deeply.

Loreen placed the photo on the desk and pulled a pointy black crystal attached to a silver chain from her pocket. She centered the picture away from all the other photos. "Now that we have a physical copy, I can use divination on it."

"Divination?" Keisha and I asked at the same time.

"I can use my obsidian as a pendulum to find the parent of Gabriel in the picture. If we find the parent, then we can find him. That might get us somewhere with all the stuff going on in this apartment." Loreen swung the necklace like a pendulum across the picture. "Our intention is important. Everyone, clear your mind and focus on finding the parent of the child."

"Even Keisha?" I was excited at being able to see the process and even more excited that Keisha could be a part of it.

"Even Keisha. Now, take a deep breath, release it slowly, and focus," Loreen said.

The pendulum swung swiftly and wildly over the entire photo, as if the wind was blowing it back and forth and in a circle. I worked to maintain my focus and deep breaths. I studied Loreen, who kept her hand steady as the pendulum started to slow in its sway. It began shortening the arc of its swing until coming to a complete stop. The point of the crystal hung over the woman standing behind Gabriel, her hands behind her back. I compared the boy to the woman and saw that they shared the same wide nose and large eyes. Even their skin was the same shade of brown.

"Is it her?" I asked.

"That's what the pendulum says," Loreen advised, placing the crystal back in her pocket.

"It's amazing we missed this before. You can tell that's his mama, for sure," I said.

Loreen picked up the picture and read the name. "Selene. It says her name is Selene Peter."

Key tapping sounded from the phone. "I found her!" Keisha shouted from the screen. "I did not know y'all have an Ibeji Village Directory. I love it." Teddy and Loreen snickered. "I found a Selene Peter that used to be listed with a Gabriel in an old directory. Maybe she's still at the address." Keisha read the address to us.

"I know that area," Teddy exclaimed, gathering up the contents of the file. "Let's go."

"I'll stay here," Keisha joked. "Let me know how it goes and what you find out."

28

My stomach was in knots. I didn't know how long I could navigate the strange events in the building. It being the site of Raymond and Reyna's disappearance didn't make this easier. The heaviness of it turned the knots into stones. Would I be next? When Mom came home from the Helper Clinic, would I still be there? Being born in Tiwa didn't stop me from feeling like an outsider. Feeling alone. Tiwa culture was different from Chicago. I couldn't imagine asking Teddy or Loreen if I could stay with them. Who knew how long it would be until all of this was figured out? Until it stopped. What if I got possessed at their house? What if there was something contagious about it and they got possessed? I couldn't risk any of that happening. I had to see this out. Mom would be returning soon. I still had no idea what had made her sick or what was going on in the apartment. My feet felt like lead as I walked just behind Teddy and Loreen. We were headed from the train station to Selene's old address.

"This is it." Teddy pointed to a small yellow house with a tiny well-kept yard in front. This neighborhood was very residential. Unlike mine, there weren't any shops within the immediate vicinity. I could only see small houses, each unique from the other. All of the lawns were well kept and it was very quiet. Being in this part of town was almost surreal. I realized my building was in a more urban part of Ibeji Village and was actually more similar to where I had grown up in Chicago. A pang of guilt shot through my body for actually liking an aspect of the building, even if it was a reminder of somewhere I missed.

Loreen gave the front door of the home three polite knocks.

"I'm coming. Give me a moment," a voice called out.

The door opened to reveal a small brown woman with long silver hair plaited down her back. She looked up at her three visitors and smiled. Her shapeless dress bore the bright colors of purple, yellow, and red. The colors started to feel like a uniform for Ibeji Village.

"Ba wo ni? How can I help you babies?" The woman's voice was as sweet and welcoming as her demeanor.

"Hi, are you Selene Peter?" Loreen asked.

"I guess that hasn't changed for over seventy years. You found me," the lady chuckled. "Why don't you come on in? I just made some tea."

Selene welcomed us in and led us to the sitting area of the tiny house. Loreen and I sat on the small green sofa across from Selene, who'd settled into an oversized matching armchair. With her tiny body, she fit like a little girl in the chair. Teddy stood behind us. Everyone waited patiently as Selene poured three tiny cups of tea on the table between her, Loreen, and I. "You sure you don't want any, young man?"

"Eshe. No."

Selene pushed two cups towards Loreen and I, holding her own and leaning back in her chair. "Now, how can I help you?" she asked while blowing her tea.

"We're doing a report on the Yardleys and we found that you used to work for them," Loreen began. "You and your son, Gabriel? We were wondering what that was like."

Selene's eyes twinkled with sadness at the mention of her son's name. "Gabriel." She put her tea back on the table and motioned Teddy towards the pictures on the wall behind him. "He used to be thick as thieves with his sister. She was a little older, but she played with him and spent time with him just as much as she could. He was devastated when she left." A morose look crossed her face as she reflected. "He loved that girl so much."

Teddy walked to the photos on the wall, scanning each of them slowly. I hoped he was looking for the little boy we saw in the pictures at my apartment. To confirm that Loreen's pendulum divination was right.

"It was my fault," Selene continued. Her eyes glistened with long-term regrets. "I just couldn't get a hold of the girl. All her dreams." She dabbed her eyes with the cloth napkin on her lap. We waited patiently for her to continue.

"And when that girl's mother died, her father got to ignoring her even more than he already did." Selene leaned forward towards us. "That's when she and Gabriel got closer. That girl used to be so sweet, but by the time Gabriel fell for her she was just as manipulative as her daddy...and vengeful too. I believe that's why Gabriel disappeared, too. Even though that girl was gone, I think he was scared of her and what she was capable of. I always thought he ran to the mainland to be with his sister and that's why he didn't come to see me." A pause. She leaned back in the chair and her voice got lower. "Or never contacted me."

"Is this your daughter, Ms. Selene?" Teddy asked from behind us. Loreen and I got up and looked at the framed photo with Gabriel and a younger version of my mom. Teddy looked at me knowingly then walked back towards his spot behind the couch. Loreen looked at the photo, nodded, and went back to sit down. I stayed a moment longer, staring in disbelief. I looked at the pictures on the wardrobe and found more of Mom and Gabriel at different stages in their lives.

"Yes, that's my oldest," Selene finished. I sat back down next to Loreen.

"You said your daughter used to be manipulative? And had something to do with Gabriel's disappearance?" Teddy asked.

Selene chuckled. "Old age got me mixing up stories. Gabriel was scared of that Yardley girl, Reyna. But I think he loved her, too. They got close in that house, even after I was let go by Mr. Yardley. She was a tricky one though. I'm almost sure she had something to do with my baby's disappearance. Nothing I know for sure though." She took a careful sip of her tea. "But Gabriel adored his sister," she continued. "They were best friends up until the day she left for the mainland. My Brena. My beautiful Brena."

I tensed up at the mention of Mom's name. I could feel Teddy watching over me.

"Thank you, I mean, Eshe." I stood up and motioned for Loreen to follow. "We appreciate your time, the tea, and helping us, Ms. Selene," I said.

"Is that all you needed for your report?" Selene asked, confused.

"Yes, that's it. Thank you, ma'am." I rushed my friends towards the door.

"A mainlander, huh?" Selene stared at me closely.

"Eshe," Loreen said with a slight bow, pushing past me.

Selene nodded and opened the door, still eyeing me. She reached out and touched my arm as I passed. "Let me know if there's anything else I can help you with." She gave my arm a gentle squeeze before letting it go. I lingered a moment before heading out the door.

"Eshe," Teddy followed me, giving a slight bow to Selene as he passed her.

I waited until we were away from the house before speaking. Anger from Mom's lack of disclosure flowed through me like electricity. Mom carried a treasure chest of secrets and I was just now finding the keys. How did I have a grandmother I'd never heard anything about? I didn't even know what I could say to Selene that would make sense to either of us. I needed all the answers. And I needed to hear them from Mom.

"I have to go see my mom. Teddy, can I have the file?"

Teddy stopped and took the file out of his backpack and handed it to me. "Loreen and I will go back to check out the apartment you stopped in front of. Reyna's old room."

"Yea, okay," I agreed. They gave me instructions on how to get to the Helper Clinic. I walked towards a different train platform without saying goodbye to them. My mind was clouded again.

29

"I think we could have gotten so much more out of Selene. Why did we leave so quickly? Was it her mom? You think she's okay?" Loreen was searching Teddy's face for anything he might know. Teddy wondered how Imani was feeling after meeting the grandmother she didn't know about, but he gave no hint to Loreen as to what was on his mind. Loreen looked to the sky instead. Teddy noticed the pinks and blues across the stretches of wispy clouds. The sun would be setting soon.

"Maybe we should come up with a plan on how to get into that apartment." She looked back to the path ahead. The top of Yardley Place revealed itself in the distance.

"I could try to break in. It's on the second floor. Maybe there's a way for me to climb in through the window from the apartment below," Teddy offered.

Loreen stifled a laugh. "I can't imagine you breaking in anywhere, Teddy. You'd definitely be seen and most people would recognize you."

A sheepish grin spread across his face. "You're probably right." He shrugged. "I can't come up with anything."

Loreen eyed the building as they got closer. She didn't know what to do either. "Let's scope out the apartment from the outside and see if anything comes to us." Teddy nodded.

One of the large ornate doors to the building was being held ajar by several packages. A woman with shortly cropped gray hair was hunched over one of the boxes, trying to slide it to the stairs inside the building.

"Can I give you a hand?" Teddy grabbed two of the boxes from the front door and brought them to the bottom of the stairs. Loreen grabbed a third box and did the same.

"Eshe." The woman wiped streams of sweat from her forehead and rested on the boxes sitting on the stairs. She was nearly as tall as Teddy and her colorful billowy pants and t-shirt stuck to odd sweaty spots on her body. Teddy thought he'd recognized the woman but couldn't place from where. He shrugged it off since he'd known so many people in Ibeji Village.

"It was going to take me a while to get them in the building, let alone in the apartment," the woman continued after catching her breath. "Will you help me carry them to my place? They're not too easy to break, but the potters can get broken, so be careful."

Teddy picked up three of the boxes, freeing the woman of any parcels, before following her up the stairs. Loreen carried the final one behind them. The woman scurried down the hall with large steps, entered her key into the door, and opened up apartment 8B- the apartment Imani had stopped in front of during her possession.

"Can I offer you some tea for your help?" She motioned for the two to come inside.

Teddy and Loreen gave each other knowing looks and nodded at the woman's offer. They couldn't help muttering gratitude to their ancestors.

30

I could finally name the feeling that welled up in me like an angry fire. My chest ached with a deep sense of hurt and abandonment. Since the day she had told me we were moving to Tiwa, I longed to know where I had come from, who I was. Mom's silence shattered that dream. I was feeling the crushing weight of my heart breaking. Heartbreak. Heartbreak caused by Mom for not telling me anything about where I was from. Heartbreak caused by someone who I thought was a friend taking advantage of me. The incident from two years ago had nothing to do with this moment except for Mom not being there for me. Just like she wasn't here for me now. I couldn't stop the same feelings from coming back. I traveled from Selene's sitting room to Mom's bedside at the Helper Clinic with adrenaline coursing through my body as I tried to put everything together. Now as I sat in the same room with her, I couldn't find the words to begin. I could only stare at the floor, my eyes watering.

Mom sat upright in the clinic bed; her arms crossed against her stomach.

"I met my grandmother today," I started, slowly raising my head to meet her fleeting looks. Mom stiffened. I planted my legs wider. I could feel heat growing in my face. I leaned in towards her.

"I also found out I have an uncle." My eyes turned cold. "Why didn't you tell me? Why didn't you ever tell me we were from Tiwa? Why am I just learning about this and I'm grown? What about my family? Your mother is all alone and I could've gotten to know her? Why would you do that to her? Why would you do that to me?" With each question, my voice got louder. I found myself standing over her, my entire body strained and rigid.

"Baby, calm down. We can talk about this. Jowo. Calm down." Mom reached her arms out towards me.

I backed away and sat in the chair. The tenseness in my shoulders forced me to sit erectly. I laughed dryly and looked away from her. "We can talk now? Why didn't we talk before? Why didn't we talk after what happened with Rome? Why haven't you ever talked to me?" I leaned back in the chair and closed my eyes. My hands clenched into tight fists.

"I am so sorry, baby. I am so sorry that I haven't been honest with you," Mom sobbed. "I regret not talking to you after what happened with Rome. When that happened to you, baby girl..." she hesitated.

"When that happened to you, it forced me to deal with things in my own past that were ugly and painful...things I wanted to protect you from. I struggled with my own past and not being able to protect you from the same pain. I didn't think I could help you. So, I shut down."

We locked eyes. A thickness grew in my throat, almost choking me.

"There is so much we do need to talk about, Imani. There are things that I have to tell you." Her words were finally full of the sincerity and openness that I needed. After all this time. I nodded curtly. I waited for a moment to see if her sincerity would fade. I had to trust that she was being real. I needed answers.

"Will you tell me about your mother and your brother?" I pulled out the picture of the Yardley Place Helpers, with Selene standing behind Gabriel. I nearly tossed the photo at her but minded my manners. "I found her through the class project I told you about. Why didn't you tell me she and Gabriel used to work for the Yardleys?" I asked.

Mom searched the picture. It seemed like she was also searching her memory for things long forgotten. "I guess I did know that, but I didn't think about it. I'd moved to the mainland not too long after my mother started bringing Gabriel with her to work."

"Why didn't you tell me that the building we live in now used to be the Yardley mansion?" My voice dripped with accusation and distrust.

Mom's eyes widened as she gasped. "I...I didn't know, baby," her voice cracked. "Everything has changed so much since I lived here. I'm so sorry, Imani. I didn't know. I didn't have time to even think about it once we moved in."

I studied my mother. For the first time, I could admit to myself that I didn't trust her. I had tried to ignore the feeling when she never wanted to talk about what had happened with Rome. Always pushing me away to the church or therapists. When I needed her- my mother. Now, I didn't know how much of what I heard was the truth. My heart broke a little more, if that was even possible. I took back the photo and stuffed it in my bag. I couldn't do this right now. It was all too much to process.

"I have to go. I'll call you later."

"Imani..."

I ignored her attempt to get me to stay. I left the Helper Clinic without looking back.

31

Then

The girl wants blood. She wants her father to feel every bit of shame, contempt, and rejection that he has inflicted upon her. She stalks to his office, slithering around, touching all of his belongings. He avoids looking at her. Instead, he stares at the blank screen of his computer. She cannot believe that he still ignores her. Even in his current state. She stops in front of his desk and picks up the picture of her mother. The only photo not of him in this room. In this whole building. She struggles against the sadness that fights to intrude at this moment. Sadness is the last of her priorities. The girl wants blood.

She slams the picture back down on the desk to get his attention. The frame falls from the desk to the floor, shattering into pieces. He manages to stop looking at the computer and turns in her direction, using just the momentum of his feet to spin the chair- since his hands are tied to the armrests. He peers past her. Through her. She can feel his dark intentions to continue hurting her. Even now.

"It's so easy, isn't it? Just ignoring me as if I am not your child. As if I am some orphan you found on your doorstep."

Silence.

"She was scared of you. You treated her horribly." Her words are drenched in bitterness and disappointment.

She rolls the chair from around the desk. The sound of glass being crushed echoes in the office.

"What's the point of staying here if you act like I don't exist?" she asks, her body tense with resentment. "Why won't you let me leave?!" she screams.

"You can leave," he replies. His voice remains calm. "You can live anywhere you want. Tiwa. The mainland. You can go. Just don't think I'll be supporting you to do whatever it is you do. I'm not wasting my money." He returns his attention to the computer screen.

Hatred and shame pulsates in harmony with her heartbeat. Tears gather. "She wasn't only scared of you. She hated you. She hated how you treated her. How you treated me. You thought she loved you?" The girl laughs loudly. She leans close to his face. "She was scared of you! She never lo-"

It takes the girl a moment to realize she is on the floor. She looks up from his pants leg, past the collar of his dashiki to see her father glaring at her, a reddened spot on his forehead from where he head butt her.

"You hit me? You hit me!" She gets upright, approaches him calmly, and grabs his chin, forcing him to meet her gaze. "You will never hurt me again. I will kill you before that happens."

He doesn't yield. "You won't do a thing."

She looks down at her father and sees him for the first time. As if a blinder has been totally removed, she understands her father will never love in the way she needs, the way she demands. While she is privileged to now see him for who he is, he will never truly see her. She feels maturity and confidence swell in her chest. She holds her head high.

"You are a coward," she says before leaving the room and slamming the door.

32

The late afternoon sun created a glare but there was Yardley Place, standing in front of me, watching me as I checked my phone for the twentieth time. Without any phone calls or text messages back from Teddy or Loreen, I headed into the building to my apartment to see if they were waiting there.

I knew I wasn't being possessed but each step to my apartment felt heavier than the last. The weight of everything I'd learned in such a short span of time burdened my body like cement blocks. I smirked. Being walked like a doll would have been an easier way to get me home. It would have required no extra effort. I sighed deeply. Everything required so much effort lately.

Loneliness tugged at me. No word from my friends and Mom still being at the Helper Clinic made the apartment feel desolate. I settled in my bedroom, reading one of my textbooks about the magic of Ibeji Village from Dr. Pike's class, skipping to the part about protection. *This is where I should have been reading from the beginning,* I chided myself. Within minutes, the words became blurry. I found more comfort from the pillow and the prospect of sleep. I napped.

A feeling, both strange and familiar, tingled throughout my body. I woke up to find myself walking slowly around my bedroom, touching and examining my stuff as though it belonged to someone else. Without my control, I went to the bedroom door and opened it, gliding out into the hallway. The sound of something being slammed down made my heart race. I tried to turn my head but my body resisted. I couldn't see where the sound had come from.

"It's so easy, isn't it? Just ignoring me as if I am not your child. As if I am some orphan you found on your doorstep." The voice coming from my mouth was not mine. I wished I could control something in my body that would stop my heart from beating out of my chest.

"She feared you. You treated her horribly," the voice continued, monotone and rote. My body paced down the hallway towards the living room. "What's the point of staying here if you act like I don't exist? Why won't you let me leave?" My face reddened with anger although I only felt fear. I stood in front of the couch, wanting so badly to sit and escape the madness. Tears gathered in my eyes. I couldn't contain the feelings of rage and shame that fully enveloped me.

"She wasn't only scared of you, she hated you. She hated how you treated her, how you treated me. You thought she loved you?" A laugh exploded from me. "She feared you! She never lo-" the voice halted. My body leaned over, bending at my waist. I felt an invisible force hit me on the forehead and knock me to the floor in front of the couch.

"You hit me? You hit me!" the voice screamed from within me. I stood with an unnatural calm, headed a few steps forward and bent over slightly again. My hand moved up to cup something unseen to me. "You will never hurt me again. I will kill you before that happens."

Tears streamed down my face. I felt a tightening in my chest. My clothes clung to me, dripping in sweat. I tried to run but my body ignored me.

My hand let go of the invisible grip. I stood upright and walked towards the front door. Soon, my head looked down at something I couldn't see. All I saw was the wooden floor.

I felt naivete ripening into profound understanding permeate my body. My head lifted and I stood tall in front of the apartment door. My hand turned the knob and opened the door.

"You are a coward," the voice calmly stated from within. I was led out of the apartment, slamming the door behind me.

I stood outside my home. I trembled. I hugged my arms to my

chest. I could move. Sweat and tears slid down my face. My clothes were soaked in sweat. I waited in the hallway, collecting myself. Calming myself. Wanting to be sure I had complete control of my body. I opened the door, stood at the threshold, and watched. I couldn't detect anything but that was no different than before. All I wanted to do was shower, change, and go to bed. I ran to the kitchen and grabbed salt. I grabbed some fresh clothes and replaced the salt that was missing from my bedroom door. How had that happened?

"You can do this, Imani. Shower then sleep. Shower then sleep. The bedroom is safe," I prepared myself. I sprinkled salt outside the bathroom door. "The bathroom will be safe," I repeated. I chuckled to myself after waiting for signs of an invisible force. *Shower then sleep.*

Eyes forward and fully focused on what needed to be done, I walked into the bathroom. Avoiding the mirror was now part of my normal routine. I turned the shower on to heat up and quickly undressed. A viscid black substance oozed out of the showerhead. Shit. I dressed in fresh clothes as quickly as I could and backed out of the bathroom.

"Ok, new plan," I muttered. "Just sleep." I thanked the Universe for making it to my bedroom without any additional incidents. My fresh sweatpants and oversized t-shirt added to my comfort. The softness and familiarity of my bed and pillow allowed me to relax. Until the sound of my stomach growling forced me to reconsider my position.

I tried to recall the last time I'd eaten. This morning? Last night? I stared at the ceiling from the comfort of my bed for another twenty minutes before I gave in to the hunger. I plotted and planned how to quickly prepare a peanut butter and jelly sandwich, grab a glass of water, and make it back to my room before anything strange began to happen. I put my shoes on to be ready for a quick escape from the apartment. *To where?* I thought to myself.

The hallway was quiet and lit by the moon from the windows high above. I moved stealthily from the doorway of my bedroom to the kitchen. *Safe.*

The hum of the refrigerator sounded louder than usual against the stillness of the apartment. I grabbed a couple of slices of bread, the jars of peanut butter and strawberry jam, and a knife. The sound of something scraping across the floor stopped me just as I was about to grab some water. I stared at my ingredients, waiting.

The scraping sound filled the room, growing longer and increasingly menacing. My heart raced as I spun around, my eyes locking onto a solitary chair sliding across the floor, closing in on me. Time seemed slow as I watched in horror, the chair gaining speed with each passing moment. Instinct kicked in, forcing me to hurl my knife aside and leap out of harm's way. I hit the ground, my knee absorbing the impact, barely having time to recover before another chair hurtled towards me. Adrenaline surged through my veins as I rolled with agility, narrowly escaping its destructive path.

I found myself nearer to the sturdy wooden kitchen table, which I seized for support. The room spun around me as I fought to steady myself, muscles straining. From the corner of my eye, I caught sight of a third chair circling the table, relentlessly pursuing me.

Without hesitation, I dashed past the oncoming chair, desperate to reach the safety of the living room. The bag lay on the couch, beckoning me, and I lunged towards it, grabbing hold. But as I made a mad dash towards the front door, a powerful gust of wind erupted, throwing me off balance. I crashed to the floor, disoriented but undeterred.

Taking a swift glance around the room, I realized with a jolt that all the windows remained tightly shut. I pulled myself up and ran towards the door. I twisted, turned, and pulled at the unlocked door, but it wouldn't budge. The strange wind in the apartment continued to blow and howl.

Fear enveloped me as an eerie voice whispered through the wind, its chilling words sending shivers down my spine. "You are home now. I have you," the unidentifiable voice moaned. The scent of morning glory filled the air, sharp and potent. The urgency to escape the confines of the building surged within me, as the force barring the door grew stronger by the second.

Closing my eyes, I bowed my head, seeking solace and guidance from my ancestors, knowing with complete confidence that they would be the ones to support me in this moment. With a trembling voice, I addressed them directly, acknowledging their unwavering presence and wisdom that guided me to this moment.

"To my ancestors that have walked with me, protected me, and illuminated my path, I am grateful for your presence and your wisdom. I trust in your guidance and honor the bond we share. Grant me the strength to face this trial, to overcome the obstacles that lie before me. Open this door that stands as a barrier between safety and the unknown. And so it is."

As I uttered these heartfelt words, a surge of energy coursed through me, amplifying my resolve. The doorknob yielded beneath my touch, loosening its grip as if responding to my plea. Taking it as a sign of their benevolence, I turned the knob and pulled the door open, propelled forward by a mixture of trepidation and self-preservation. I ran down the stairs to apartment 1B. The sound of my fists banging on the door rang throughout the lobby, accompanying my calls to Ellie. There was no reply. I couldn't wait. My feet carried me faster than they ever had in my life as I ran out of the building.

33

I walked mindlessly, unaware of the rain. Or I didn't care. Rain splashed onto my head from awnings and the exposed sky. Most of the stores I passed were either preparing to close or had already done so. The night's events played at the back of my mind. I tried pushing them down as soon as they came up.

How's this been working out for you? I thought to myself, realizing that my go-to solution for most of my problems was just to not think about them. Not acknowledge them. *Never want to deal with it. Always running. Just like your mother.* I trembled with feelings I could no longer contain. The tears I couldn't hold back any longer fell down my face in rivers. The rain grew with my tears. I walked and cried without a destination. Until I had one.

The botanica's open sign welcomed me. I stood in front of the dark glass door covered by an awning and checked my reflection. A gentle wipe with the bottom of my dampened t-shirt cleared the tears and rain from my face, but there was nothing I could do about the tears that stayed pooled in my eyes. The floodgate had opened.

Bells jingled when I opened the door, alerting Malini, the shop-keeper, to my presence. "Ba wo ni?" she sang. "It's a late night." She poked her head from behind a curtain and waved at me before going back behind the curtain.

I nodded, thoughtlessly. I wandered the store, fingering objects without really looking at them. It must have been a few minutes when

I realized I was standing among the herbs holding the morning glory packaged in a small violet pot.

"Ah. I remember you." She was standing next to me, restocking some of her goods. She was also snake free this time. "You were interested in the morning glory before. When you were with your friends."

"I smelled it. I smelled it again," I said under my breath.

Malini stopped her task, tilted her head, and made direct eye contact with me. "Are you okay, baby?" She faced me squarely. "What happened?"

I let the damn break and wept uncontrollably. She waited patiently for me, rubbing my arm from time to time.

I bit down on my lower lip, my tears subsiding. Malini produced a bright multi-colored cloth from one of the pockets on her floor-length skirt and offered it to me. I smiled weakly and took it.

"Thank you," I whispered, cleaning my face.

"*Jowo*, come with me."

Malini guided me to the curtains and held them open, waving me through. On the other side was a room green with plants. The plants filled every corner and empty wall space. Where there were no plants, there was a couch and a small dining table. I found the snake in its glass cage, watching me from a shelf nearly hidden by plants.

"Have a seat." She pointed towards the table, walked to a small fridge hidden among the plants and pulled out a glass pitcher of a purple drink. From a hutch covered with hanging ivy, she pulled two glasses. Malini poured the drink into the glasses, placed one in front of me, the other near her seat, and replaced the pitcher back into the small fridge. "Lavender lemonade," she said, joining me at the table and drinking hers. "It'll help you feel better. It'll help you relax."

The drink cooled my body down slowly as it moved past my tongue, down my throat, and into my stomach. The tanginess and sweetness of the drink confused my senses but the lavender calmed them. It soothed my entire being. I finished the drink without stopping.

"Thank you. It was good." I rubbed the back of my neck. "I mean, *Eshe*."

Malini waved the sentiment away. "You are quite welcome, baby. Now tell me when you smelled the herb."

I twisted a single braid around my finger and staved off a feeling of nausea. I didn't want to recount any of this but knew I had to get it out.

"I live in Yardley Place. So many strange things have been happening since we moved in. I think even my mom getting sick had something to do with the apartment." I unwrapped and wrapped the braid. "Twice, I've smelt the morning glory. The second time was tonight. After I was possessed- again- a strange voice was telling me it had me and then the apartment wouldn't let me out. Until I prayed."

Malini raised her eyebrows. She got up and poured me another glass of lemonade. "Morning glory has many magical uses," she started. "Firstly, it is poisonous. Which is why I sell it with a warning label. It can be used for attraction to something or someone. That's why most people use it now...if they use it at all. In an older time, it was used to bind someone. Or even banish them. For those purposes, you need a poppet. Folks don't really make poppets like they used to."

We sipped our drinks in tandem.

"What's a poppet?" I slid my chair closer to the table.

"It's a doll made to represent someone. Most folks make their own poppets. But if you're up to no good," she shook her head dramatically, "you make someone else's poppet. A poppet that represents that person. And you can use magic on that poppet to affect the person." She blinked slowly and drank more. "Gotta have a piece of them in the poppet though. It's harder to do without that person knowing."

I frowned at my empty glass. I pressed my lips together in lieu of asking for more.

"Would you like a reading, child? On the house." Malini pulled a box covered in a white silk cloth from a shelf that was hidden by more plants. Out of the box, she took a colorful deck of cards, slightly larger than playing cards. The back of the cards had a gold geometric design atop a purple space. She shuffled the cards and laid them to the side. From another shelf, she produced a bag of cornmeal. She poured some into her hand and sprinkled it onto the center of the table into an intricate design. I crossed my arms away from the table and watched the shopkeeper shape the cornmeal into a heart divided in half by a straight line with complex curly lines extending from the top and bottom of the straight line. She added a simple dagger to the side of the heart and filled the inside with four sweeping arcs, two on each side of the heart. As she drew with the cornmeal, she murmured a prayer that I couldn't hear clearly.

"Take the deck and cut it," Malini said softly, lifting the deck over the cornmeal drawing and placing it in front of me. I separated it into two decks, placed one on top of the other and put both back on the table, away from the design. She picked it up and laid the top three cards face up in front of me, on top of the cornmeal heart.

She pointed at the first card. It pictured a brown-skinned woman sitting in front of a mirror. She held a fan that covered nearly all her face. The woman wore long white gloves and was seated in front of a peacock. She was the epitome of grace.

"This card is Oshún," Malini started. "When called upon, Oshún can bring love into your life. But this is not about love. This is about strong emotions becoming something solid in this realm. And this card," she pointed to the card in the middle. A wounded warrior carried his shield and sword. A fire raged behind him. "It represents the regret that will come after a war is waged."

I followed her finger to the final card. This card displayed multiple black male figures. The three foremost in the front had their faces painted as skulls, wore top hats, and smoked cigars.

"These are the barons," Malini said. "They represent the performance of life and, for this reading, that means there will be an unexpected turn of events."

I nodded and studied each of the cards, working to come up with my own interpretation. Another part of magic I would have to learn about...if I survived all this. Malini looked deep into my eyes, again. "If this reading was for you, I would say that love is coming your way. If you are willing to put up the fight inside of you. And, if you are, it will be unlike anything you have ever experienced."

She maintained her stare and lifted the cards from the cornmeal. "But this reading is not for you. I know from your aura you have been possessed. And the person, or persons, that have possessed you are not quite amongst the land of the spirits. They may not even be part of the land of the living." With one swoop, Malini used her arm to sweep the cornmeal to the floor. "This reading means that there is a war going on right now. And you are caught in the middle. The war is among family. It started as a fight for love but has turned into something very dark." She grabbed my hands into her own and squeezed them firmly, still holding my eyes with her own. "But I can help you."

34

Thursday

Teddy rolled over, ready to hit the alarm. He was perturbed that he'd woken up early enough to beat the alarm, but he was up. He turned his head too quickly and the room started to spin. He closed his eyes for a moment and opened them when he felt better. This wasn't his room. Someone shifted next to him and moaned. He got a whiff of lavender. He didn't want to risk his head spinning again and called out instead.

"Loreen?" The name felt heavy on his tongue.

"Teddy?" He could hear her clearly and wondered if she shared the same sick feeling. "Where are we?" she asked, the words clawing their way out her mouth.

Teddy searched the room for clues of their whereabouts. They lay on a blue couch that he knew he'd seen before. The red and black checkered ceiling surprised him. "We're at Imani's."

"E-man-ee's!" Loreen had returned to her normal self. Teddy chuckled. "What are we doing at Imani's? Where is she? How did we get here?" she asked.

Teddy sat up slowly, searching his mind for the previous night's events. "What's the last thing you remember?"

Loreen was upright, holding her head in her hands. "I don't know.

I think talking to Imani's friend, Keisha, while we were searching for more info. Then we visited that lady."

Teddy, now fully sitting, looked around the room for any other signs. He remembered talking with Keisha and Imani, looking at the file, even leaving Selene's house...

"I can't remember anything after that. What did we do?" He attempted to keep his voice light. "Imani?" His deep voice echoed through the apartment to no response.

"She's not here." Loreen squeezed her temples. "My head hurts. How do you feel?" She found her purse still on her shoulder and started searching for relief.

"As long as I don't move too quickly, I'm okay. Were we drugged?" Teddy watched as Loreen checked her pants and blouse for any signs of damage. His heart dropped as he thought about what it must be like as a woman to have those fears. Fears he didn't really have to think about. "I don't know. I don't feel like we weren't," he joked. "Imani?" he tried to call out again, his voice cracking. The two waited, listening for any signs of Imani.

A key turned in the lock of the apartment door, breaking their concentration. Teddy rushed to stand up in front of Loreen but found himself back on the couch next to her. His head swirled. He shut his eyes to recenter himself, then opened them as the doorknob clicked. He stared at the door and gulped.

35

⚜

I walked into my apartment with a large shopping bag, simply labeled "Botanica." Teddy released a shaky laugh.

"What are you guys doing here? How did you get in?" I asked. I dropped the bag and rushed over to them. I reached down and lifted Teddy's face to mine. "Are you okay?"

Loreen sat back on the couch and closed her eyes. "Do you have anything for a headache?"

I let go of Teddy's face and hurried to the kitchen. "My mom always makes me this tea when I get a headache," I called out. "It works pretty quickly for a natural remedy." I found ginger in the fridge and started preparing it. "What happened to you two?"

Teddy joined me in the kitchen. I could tell he was pushing himself to not appear as weak as he probably felt. He pulled forward the chair from the middle of the room and scooted it next to the table. Loreen followed shortly after, still holding her head in place.

"What's the last thing you remember us doing?" Loreen asked.

Water splashed out of the kettle as it overfilled. I turned back to the task at hand. "You two were going to check out that apartment. Apartment 8B. I couldn't get in contact with you after I visited my mom. That was hours ago. So much has happened since then...for me."

Teddy pulled his cell phone from his pocket and checked the time. "It's nearly 2 a.m. How long have we been here? Wait. Did you go back to the shop?"

I examined their faces for the concern and confusion I expected them to have from not remembering anything. "Are you two okay?"

Teddy waved his hand nonchalantly, pausing Loreen's response. "Just tell us what happened to you. It may give us some clues."

I explained the scene I was possessed to act out and the other strange happenings that occurred in the apartment that had forced me to leave. Loreen eyed the chairs scattered around the kitchen. Her trepidation swelled in her silence. She had to feel how I did, waking up in a strange place. I reached out for her then drew my hand back when she spoke.

"And you still came back? After nasty sludge came out of the shower?" she asked. She opened her mouth to say more, then closed it and shook her head approvingly. She inspected the kitchen further.

I nodded. "After going to the botanica and meeting with Malini, the shopkeeper, I feel like I can handle this. She told me some things that I think will help us get rid of the dark energy here." I placed two empty mugs with teaspoons in front of each of them and filled them with steaming hot tea. "Let's help you with those headaches, first. Then we can talk about a plan."

Loreen leaned back in her seat. Teddy blew at each spoonful of tea before taking a sip. I joined them at the table and described the reading I had received from the shopkeeper. I left out the part about me finding a love that would change my life. No need to stray from the business at hand. I only mentioned the war she described.

"A war? Between who?" Teddy asked.

"Maybe the Yardleys and someone who owed them money," Loreen offered.

"I don't know that yet. She said it came from love and evolved into war. Maybe," I looked past my friends, "maybe, it was the boy, Gabriel."

Teddy made eye contact with me. "That could be why you're involved," he whispered.

I nodded.

"What do you mean?" Loreen looked at us for answers.

"What it means is that I need to start practicing magic." I took

Teddy's empty cup and placed it in the kitchen sink. "If we're going to learn what's really going on in this building and get rid of this negative energy, I must be a part of it. Malini gave me some ideas for using herbal magic once we find out what's behind this."

"We're going to need more than that," Loreen interrupted. She tested the coolness of her tea. "We need to talk with Dr. Pike. She is one of the experts on the magic of Ibeji Village."

"We can talk to her after class tomorrow." Teddy sounded excited. "I mean today." He moaned a bit.

Loreen and I laughed. "We should get some sleep," I offered.

"Yes," Loreen said, inspecting the kitchen a final time. "But not here. Imani, you can come to my place."

I beamed. It was a huge offer in Tiwa to allow someone to stay in your home. Tiwans were big on surrounding themselves with the right energy. That included guests in their home. Especially guests that would sleep in their home. The offer meant that Loreen trusted me and my energy. It also meant that I could sleep and get ready for school without worrying about what would happen next.

Teddy got up from the table and took a step back. Loreen stood and looked at her watch. "Ok, let's go. But don't bring too much from this place. I don't want you haunting up my house."

Teddy and I exchanged a glance and laughed.

36

At one point during the lecture, I thought my foot might fall off from tapping it so much. My impatience turned to relief when class ended. Teddy, Loreen, and I all rushed to the front of the room to speak with Dr. Pike.

"Aw, the three amigos," Dr. Pike greeted us. "Any updates about Imani's adventures at Yardley Place?"

"We can't remember ours," Teddy replied. "We found the mother of the boy and went back to explore the building more but Loreen and I woke up in Imani's apartment in the middle of the night."

"That was after they stopped me from a possession," I added.

Dr. Pike closed the laptop in front of her and looked at each of our faces with a pained gaze.

I shared with her what I had learned from Malini. "We need your help, Dr. Pike. I need your help with magic," I finished.

Dr. Pike nodded. "I can do that. I can help." She circled us cautiously with her hand holding her face. "I shouldn't have let you do this on your own."

I eyed her, my head cocked to the side. She took a deep breath. "Not many things make me nervous, Imani. I've been all over Tiwa excavating and entrenched in the magic. Not even Omi Lake and the Statue of Nkisi brought me as much fear as the tales I've heard about Yardley Place. I have to admit that I was scared. You see, once I arrived in Tiwa, the tales of this building was some of the first lore I encountered. The first time I heard the story-"

144

"Dr. Pike," Loreen spoke softly. "What do you suggest?" The professor stopped back at the podium.

"Yes, yes. Of course. Progress has indeed been made by you three. You seem to be well on your way to figuring out what is going on and perhaps what happened to Raymond and Reyna Yardley. Yes. Yes. On the subject of magic, you should always start with a protection spell. I then suggest that the use of a road opening spell is put into place. Once that is used," she stiffened, "the other remains to be seen."

We chattered about not knowing how to do a road opening spell. "I've got protection down. That's nothing," Loreen added, clutching the lone crystal around her neck.

"Oh, well, no worries. I will go with you to Imani's apartment to help. Allow me a moment to gather some things from my home, settle my family, and I will join you. Teddy and Loreen, you should gather your familiars. We'll all meet at the platform."

37

"Mom?" I ran from the doorway to Mom standing at the threshold of the kitchen. She stopped waving a burning bundle of herbs around and hugged me tightly, holding the herbs above her head.

"Babygirl!"

"When did you get home?"

"Long enough to start a protection spell on the home and start cleansing it," she replied, releasing me from her grip. Her eyes were twinkling. "I appreciate you keeping my altar clean." Mom turned to the strangers in her home, honing in on Teddy. "Hello again, young man."

Dr. Pike stepped up in front. "Ba wo ni? I am Dr. Yvonne Pike, a professor at Ibeji Village Community College. Your daughter and these two are in my History of Tiwa class."

"This must be some school project for you to come to my home," Mom interrupted.

"It wasn't exactly a school project, Mom. This is Loreen and her gecko, Irarian. You remember Teddy and his dog Adu. Everyone's been helping me with some of the things going on in this building."

"Ah huh." She still held on to the herb bundle. Sage. I finally recognized it from when she used to wave it around our home in Chicago.

"Ba wo ni? Ms. Brena. It's nice to see you again." Teddy scratched his head and smiled sheepishly. Adu gave Mom a quick sniff before laying down at her feet.

"Ms. Bennett," Loreen stepped around the dog and the rest of the group. "We have so much to tell you. Imani has been braver than I could ever be. We've just been trying to support her with all the...weird-ness. Even weirder than normal in Tiwa." Loreen's face twitched as she laughed uncomfortably. I couldn't believe we'd gotten to the point where she was complimenting me unsolicited.

"Ba wo. So, it's not a school project?" Mom asked.

The three guests and I clamored over each other as we each tried to explain what we knew and shared everything we'd witnessed.

"Wait!" Mom waved her free hand. We stopped to watch Mom walk to the kitchen with her herbs and returned empty handed. "I see I've missed a lot. I do want to know everything. Please, everyone, have a seat." She waved towards the couch. "I need to speak with Imani first," she continued, turning to face me. "Baby girl, let's go in my room and talk."

Dr. Pike, Teddy, and Loreen sat on the couch in an awkward silence. I walked past Adu puttering over to Teddy's feet and slumping down beside them. "So should we plan?" Teddy asked the other two. "Or we should wait?"

"You should wait," Mom called from down the hall. "Make yourselves at home. Food and drinks are in the kitchen."

"Make yourselves at home with dark spirits. Mm mm," Loreen's voice carried down the hall.

"Might as well eat," Teddy's followed.

* * *

How long had Mom been back? Her sheets were freshly changed and the altar had fresh water in the bowl with a purple flower resting on top. She'd opened the window slightly, bringing in a small breeze. A small shiver slid down my spine. I remembered the voice that had carried on the breeze. I went to the window and shut it before joining Mom as she kneeled at her altar.

"You've never asked me about the people in these pictures." She lifted a black and white photo of a woman that she somewhat resembled. Before Selene's time, I guessed. She studied the picture for a moment, then placed it back. She turned to me. "I know you have questions. You deserve answers."

I pulled my legs to the side and gave her the chance to speak.

"There are so many things that you deserve to know. Before we venture down the path of what's going on in this home, you need to know these things." Mom turned to face me, then looked down at her empty hands.

"Mom?"

"Gabriel is my brother. We were close as he was growing up. My mother and I though, we just fought all the time. Especially after she had Gabriel. The arguments got worse. They got bigger. One day, we got into a big argument. I can't even remember how it started. But it got physical. One of us struck first and the other responded." Mom shook her head. "I don't even remember the details. But, I couldn't face anyone after that. I couldn't believe I hit my mom. I felt so much shame. I tried to justify to myself that it wasn't my fault, that my mother was to blame. Yet, all I found were reasons why it was my fault. So, I moved to the mainland. I left my family without saying goodbye. It was hard at first, not communicating with them. Then the more time that passed, the easier it was. I just told myself that they wouldn't want to hear from me anymore."

Mom paused and stared at the ceiling. "I should have told you that we were from Tiwa sooner. I was scared of what feelings it would bring up for me if I did. I was scared of coming back and facing my family. I didn't know what my mother told Gabriel. I realize now that he trusted me, but by then I'd grown used to being without my family- especially my mom." She met my wide eyes. "If I had told you, I knew that all you would want was to come back."

"But we did come back," I uttered.

Mom nodded. "I wonder if I was trying to encourage you to run from your problems by bringing you back. By forcing me to deal with mine."

I slid away from her. "What about my dad, Mom? Is that what the argument was about?"

She shook her head gently and ran her finger down my braids. "No, baby girl. But I also haven't been honest with you about that." She covered her face with her hands, took a deep breath and then removed them. "I'm not your birth mother."

<h1 style="text-align:center">38</h1>

❧

Then

The girl walks into her father's office with a bulging belly and a tray of food. She places the tray on the side table and smiles at the room's only occupant sitting bound and gagged in the office chair. He follows her with his eyes as she comes close to him.

"I brought you some food, Daddy. Some water, too." She reaches for the end of the tape that covers his mouth. "This may hurt a little." He squints his eyes and braces himself as she rips it off. He reopens his eyes to find the moisture in them and his daughter playfully examining the tape. "I got some of your mustache with that. I'm sorry," she says with an exaggerated pout.

"Reyna..." he calls her name.

"O! So you do know my name," she interrupts, preparing a spoonful of food. "It's not 'that girl' or 'your daughter.'" She shoves the spoon into his mouth. Sauce drips from his lips to his clothes. "It's not like you ever really spoke to me directly," she says, forcing more food into his mouth. Soon, his dingy dashiki top and linty pants sport the red tomato sauce in colorful splotches.

"The way you spoke about me to my mother. Psh. The way you spoke to my mother." She walks back to the tray and replaces the plate of food with a glass of water. "Open up." Water splashes down his gullet and all over his clothes, adding to the avant-garde essence of his clothing.

"Jowo," he begs. "One avoids danger at the early stage."

"What you give, you get," she says. Reyna places the glass back on the tray and grabs one of the other chairs from the office. "You know what this reminds me of? Do you remember?"

It takes her a moment to sit comfortably. Her arm resting on the chair to hold up the weight of her body as she rests and settles in the chair. The heaviness of her belly forces her to lean into the chair, instead of sitting straight up in it. "Do you remember after that dinner party when you forbade my mother to see me? When, for weeks, you told all the Helpers to not speak to me when they brought me my food?" Reyna lets out strange, nearly forced, laughter. "Doesn't that remind you of this?"

Raymond keeps his eye on the daughter he ignored and chastised for most of her childhood. She was nearly an adult now and still almost a twin for her mother. Except for the rage that dominated her. That was nothing like her mother. He can't remember the specific event she speaks about. He bows his head as he realizes how much he put his own flesh and blood through. He feels shame but it is fleeting.

"Don't remember? I guess not. Maybe it's not that much like back then after all. Because I'm actually talking to you." She rubs her pregnant belly and breathes deeply. She believes she sees pity in her father's face. "Don't feel sorry for me, Daddy. I'm okay." Her rubs are gentle and slow. She fingers the baby's toes as it kicks through. "Do you know how easy it has been to manage your businesses? Whew, Daddy. These people do not care for you." Another strange laugh. "It's like they were relieved when they didn't have to deal with you. Especially when I let the Helpers go. A nice last paycheck, no questions asked. They skipped out of here, smiling and laughing, ready for the happiness they deserve." The laugh begins to fill the room in haunting chords and choruses. "Soon, I'll be skipping out of here. Getting the happiness I deserve. Living the life I should have been allowed to live. As soon as I've sold all the real estate you had in Ibeji Village. I'm almost there," she says with a wink.

A slight knock at the door precedes its opening. The boy enters the room. A frown seems permanent on his face, along with the dark circles under his eyes. He avoids the man he helped bind and instead focuses on Reyna. There is nothing he can do to hide the glow on his face and twinkle in his eyes when he looks at her. "How are you feeling, love? Maybe you should go lay down. Extra stress isn't good for the baby," he says to the girl.

Reyna looks over to her lover, unable to wipe the look of hate from her face. The boy steps back from the power and force of her gaze. If he hadn't been there the whole time, he might have mistaken that look as meant for him. He knows her heart.

"I'm okay, Gabriel. I don't feel stressed at all," she nearly sings. She returns her stare to her father. "I haven't felt better. I know what we have to do next. Like I said, Daddy. Soon. Soon, I'll be leaving. When I go...you go." The laugh she releases drives Gabriel out of the room. The laugh makes Raymond's body heave with tears.

39

"You're not my mom? I don't understand." I got up. Breathing became difficult. I felt pain in my chest. I paced back and forth. From the bed to the window. The window to the bed. Interrupting the sunbeams that snuck in through the slightly parted curtain pleats. I searched the floor for answers, trying to make sense of everything.

"Come. Sit with me." Mom stopped me mid-step, grabbed my hand, and pointed to the bed. "I need to tell you everything. Everything I know."

I sat down reluctantly, facing the wall opposite her. "Everything you know?" I asked. Disbelief and anger danced around my words.

I could hear Mom rubbing her arms. "Before we moved into this apartment- before we moved to Tiwa- I wasn't completely sure that Reyna was your mother." Her voice shifted, as if she was talking to my back. "Gabriel came to the mainland with this sweet, beautiful baby girl. He didn't tell me anything about Raymond or Reyna. He only asked me to keep the baby safe. He said he'd be back soon after taking care of some things. He said you wouldn't be safe with him while he did it."

I could hear the sadness in her voice.

"I knew Gabriel. I saw in his face that he wasn't going to come back. I had to change your name to keep you safe. I contacted a friend from Tiwa who had also moved to the mainland. She helped to get you a mainlander birth certificate. We gave you a new name and birthdate."

Silence. I could feel her watching the back of my head.

"You changed my name. What's my name? When is my real birth-day?" I whispered.

More silence. More sadness.

"Ruby," she said. "Your name is Ruby. And I don't know your true birthdate."

I jumped up from the bed. I finally had clarity. It all made sense. "Reyna is my mother. She has to be. It must be her in the visions. That's why I thought it was me." I shook my head. "I look like...my mother."

I turned around and met Mom's gaze. Tears streaked down both of our faces. "Mom." I reached out for her hand.

She cried harder. She walked around to me, reached up, and pulled my head down in a hug.

"I'm so sorry I didn't tell you anything before. You're my child and I didn't want you to think otherwise."

I hugged her back. My words were stuck in my throat. My thoughts danced all over the place. Mom wasn't my mom. The boy in the pictures was my dad. So, Mom was my aunt.

The clearer everything got, the murkier it seemed.

"I know you're confused, baby girl. I know this is a lot." She held onto me, rubbing my back and stroking my head as she sobbed. The secrets I desperately needed her to share with me sat between us like an old friend long waiting to be acknowledged. I felt lighter. As if all the shortened conversations, unanswered questions, and half-truths became complete, acknowledged and honest.

I let go of all my curiosities. All the fear that held me back from moving forward. Of the heartbreak that had nearly consumed me until now. Tears flowed out like a river of pain, long waiting to be released. We stood holding each other until I could let go of everything that wasn't a part of my spirit. Until I set myself free from all the energy I'd taken in. All the energy that didn't belong to me. I could rebuke the heartache caused by not knowing who I was. I could start to move past the heartbreak that came from trusting the wrong person. I released all the pent-up emotion that had been building over the last two years up until this moment. And my mother held me through it. I was ready to move forward.

"I really have to tell you what's been going on," I said, stepping back from Mom. I wiped my face. She grabbed a cloth off her dresser and helped me. "Now that it makes more sense."

"Go on," she said, dabbing at my cheeks.

"Things have been strange ever since we moved here. I've had strange visions. I was in the basement and thought I was looking at me and a strange woman. I saw myself in the room with who I think was my father." I shuddered. "I thought maybe I was inserting myself into these visions, but now I think it may have been my...It was Reyna."

"What kind of visions?" Mom's face had the combined look of being inquisitive and knowledgeable.

I explained the scenes I had witnessed in the basement and in the apartment when it had been Raymond's office. I added details of my possessions, when I was unable to control my body and pranced around the apartment, then forced to act out something that I couldn't see. I described all the strange things that had happened in the building, including the voices, my monster reflection, and sludge coming from the shower.

"Oh my stars, Imani. Why didn't you tell me about this when you visited me? Or called me to tell me." Shock was the dominant expression on her face now.

I shook my finger in tandem with my conclusions. "I think you getting sick had something to do with it. You did strange things too before the Helpers came. I found you contorted and catatonic. You were mouthing words that another voice was speaking. Once you were at the clinic, you were okay. I didn't want you rushing back home until I figured out what was going on."

Mom nodded and hugged me again. "My sweet, courageous baby girl. I love that you were protecting me. But, you didn't have to do this alone. I could've helped you once I came home."

I moved away from her, shook my head, and straightened my stance. How could I explain how scared I was? Not just for me but for her. I had to figure this out as soon as I could. I knew I could do it without her, but did she believe that I was capable? Did she see my strength? "I wasn't alone, Mom. We're not alone. My friends have been helping me. I even met the owner of a botanica that helped me too. I know where to start now."

She studied my face. Through her eyes, I felt the electricity of Tiwa's essence surging through me, pushing me to grow. Preparing me for tribulations. Cultivating my power. Through her eyes, I felt her really see me. I knew she recognized the woman I had grown into in just some days. I saw concern and pride swell within her. She didn't say anything, though. Just, "Okay. Let's go back with your friends."

40

"Are you ok?" Teddy stood from the kitchen table when he saw us come back. He must've noticed the puffiness and redness of my eyes. They were a matching pair to my mom's.

I nodded. "I'm fine." I paused, thoughtfully. "Things make more sense now. I understand why I've been going through all of this in this building."

"What do you know, Imani?" Dr. Pike chimed in. She stood from where she was sitting at the kitchen table drinking tea next to Teddy and slid her chair in offering to Mom. Mom took it and quietly thanked the professor with a quick bow of her head. Loreen sat on the other side of Teddy, continuing to pet Adu.

I looked at my mom. She nodded.

"My mom just told me that she's not my birth mother. Gabriel is my father. Not my uncle." I couldn't believe I was telling all my family business so nonchalantly. But, it had to be said for us to resolve things. Any other situation not involving evil reflections and possessions, I might've waited a little longer to share the information.

Silence echoed through the apartment. Loreen gasped. "So, Selene is your grandmother?"

"Yes," I said. Loreen smiled gently in reply. I could see her putting the pieces together of why we had left Selene's home so abruptly. "And we think," I took a deep breath and continued, "that Reyna is my mother."

"Ooooooh." Teddy's jaw dropped.

"You're a Yardley?" Dr. Pike called out. She inched closer to where

I stood. She reached out to touch me, reconsidered, and put her hand down.

I extended my hand, touched Dr. Pike's shoulder, and nodded. "I think the visions I've been seeing haven't been me. It's been Reyna."

"What about the possessions? The other strange things in the apartment? Our loss of memory?" Teddy shot out the questions all at once without taking a breath.

"I haven't that figured out, yet." I walked to the couch where I'd left the bag from the botanica. "But Malini, the shopkeeper, gave me some insight on how we can all find out more."

I took the bag into the kitchen, pulled out the contents, and placed them on the table. Dr. Pike stood from the table and examined each of the items more carefully.

"A mirror, white cloth, white candles, silk pouches, and..." she said. She picked up three small bags of herbs and sniffed them individually. "Lavender. Sage. Mugwort." Dr Pike picked up and placed back down an incense burner and charcoal without calling out their name. "Scrying," she said simply.

"Yes," I confirmed. "Malini did a reading for me. She told me that whatever is haunting me is involved in some type of war. She also said they are in between the living and the dead." I described the cards containing Oshún, the wounded warrior, and the barons and the meaning the shopkeeper had given to them in her divination.

"Ah, yes," Dr. Pike said. "From the pulling of the barons, it seems you have met a Voodoo practitioner. Voodoo has long been a tradition of both the descendants on the mainland and Tiwa. Not many practitioners here in Tiwa, but it seems you were able to meet one. You see, Imani. Many elements of the different magic of the descendants are shared. Oshún, you see..."

"Excuse me, Dr. Pike," Loreen said politely to Dr. Pike then turned to face me. "Imani, you want to use the mirror for scrying? To see what's haunting you?" Loreen's tone with me had changed. Instead of snippy and condescending, she seemed to respect and admire me. I was relieved to work with her instead of against each other. I would need her magic, as well as everyone else's.

"I want all of us to use the mirror for scrying. We'll also need to put protection in place from whatever is in this apartment so we can practice the ritual undisturbed."

"Of course we'll help," Teddy offered. "Adu, door," he commanded. The dog trotted over to the door and sat watching it.

Dr. Pike and Loreen nodded at Mom and me. I rummaged through the kitchen drawer, located scissors, went back to the table and picked up the white cloth. It rolled out and spread onto the floor when I held it up high.

"Mom," I called out. Without additional instruction, she came and helped me stretch the cloth out onto the table. I cut the cloth into about one-yard pieces. Mom took each piece as it was cut and handed it to the guests. The group needed no directions. Loreen put her braids into a bun, covered her head with the cloth, and twisted the remaining cloth around the bun. Teddy, Dr. Pike, and Mom covered their heads and looped their extra cloth into a crown around their heads. I put my braids into a bun on the top of my head and wrapped the white cloth around my head until the wrap was secure and all my hair was covered.

Dr. Pike positioned the chairs around the kitchen table. She took the mirror and positioned it on the table at an angle so each of the chairs could be seen in it. Mom began filling the silk pouches with lavender and sage and handed one to everyone. I lit the charcoal inside the incense burner and then the candles while I waited for the charcoal to get a good burn. I placed the candles in a semi-circle around the mirror. We each chose our seats. Loreen sat on the end, next to Teddy-who held my chair for me. Mom sat next to me and Dr. Pike at the other end. We all naturally spread into a semi-circle, each of us in front of one of the candles.

"Thank you, Teddy," I said as I sprinkled the mugwort onto the burning charcoal and took my seat.

Mom brought out a bottle of Florida water and sprinkled some on her hands before passing it to Dr. Pike. She rubbed it into her hands while Dr. Pike did the same and reached around Mom to pass it to me so the rest of us could do the same.

"Mom, will you pray?"

"Not quite, baby girl. First-" Mom started.

"First, we need to meditate and jointly clear our heads to enter the spiritual plane," Dr. Pike interrupted. "We jointly chant to begin with until we get there. It's not really a prayer so much, but rather-"

"Thank you, Dr. Pike," I cut her off. "How about you start the chant?"

My mom caught my eyes and grinned. In any other situation, I knew she would lecture me about respecting my elders and not cutting them off. In this situation, though, she was letting me be the leader. She probably also agreed that Dr. Pike tended to be long winded.

41

The group acted as one. Even our inhales and exhales were united. Candlelight flickered, making shadows prance around the room and on our faces. We held hands and chanted in unison, but each person focused on the candle in front of them. Soon, the individual candles disappeared and we were standing in Raymond's office, as it had been nearly twenty years ago. I squeezed Mom's hand. She returned the gesture.

"It's okay, baby," she whispered. "This is the past. We cannot be harmed here. We are protected both here and in our bodies. Also, nothing we do here will impact what has already happened."

"In our bodies?" I shrilled under my breath.

"Yes," Dr. Pike replied, her timbre matching mine and Mom's. "Our minds are on a different plane, but our bodies are still where we left them. You see, with the group use of scrying-"

"Look over there. In that chair." Teddy lifted his and Loreen's hand and pointed to someone sitting bound and gagged in the office chair.

"Someone's coming," Loreen hissed.

Everyone but me gasped as Reyna stomped into the room. Her stride was hindered by the girth of her belly. No one could mistake the fury in her steps.

"Imani, is that...?" Mom called out.

"That's Reyna," I answered.

"I can see why you thought it was you," Loreen chimed in. "You look just like her."

I looked over at Mom. Her face didn't change as she watched the scene unfold in front of them. "Gabriel," she whispered.

I turned towards the entrance to see a young, worn-out Gabriel enter the room. His shoulders were hunched over as he headed to the man tied up in the chair.

"Roll him into the cellar," Reyna commanded. Gabriel did as he was told, speaking to the man in hushed tones.

"What did he say?" Loreen asked the group. "He just whispered something to the man. That's Raymond, right?"

"He said, 'I'm sorry,'" Teddy replied.

Gabriel pushed the man right past us. We examined the man in the chair as closely as we could. "That IS Raymond Yardley," Dr. Pike called out. "Let's follow. Remember to keep holding hands."

We walked in a single file line holding hands down the long vermillion hallway. Reyna was already steps ahead of us and Gabriel pushing Raymond.

"She's moving so fast for being so pregnant," Teddy noticed. "I can't believe that's you in there, Imani."

I knew I was looking at my birth mother carrying me but I understood that I needed to focus on ending the phenomena that centered around me. I chose not to respond. I could process all of this later.

"Look what they have done with the place." Dr. Pike studied the building. "I can tell where a lot of the changes were made to turn this into Yardley Place. Yet, they left a lot of the original building."

Gabriel stopped at the top of the flight of stairs that led down to the main floor. "What about the stairs?" he called out. Reyna stopped halfway down the stairs and glared at her lover.

"Figure it out."

"This must've been before the elevator was put in," Mom whispered.

"I'm so sorry," Gabriel repeated to Raymond. We watched as Gabriel turned the chair around and walked backwards down the stairs, bouncing the chair down each step. Raymond still didn't speak. His head hung down, his chin slapping against his chest as they made their way down the staircase. No one said it out aloud, but we were all concerned for his well-being. I was hoping that this didn't turn out the way it looked. With Raymond either dead or seriously injured.

"Watch your step," Dr. Pike called out. We started behind Gabriel, carefully walking as we held hands. Once at the bottom, Gabriel rolled Raymond towards Reyna. She waited at an open door that led to another flight of stairs. The same door that led to the basement in present day. Gabriel turned the chair backwards again and got Raymond down the same way, bouncing in his chair. We were right behind them.

The cellar was larger than the present-day basement that I had ventured to. I recalled my first experience seeing this room as it was, when it held a playroom for Reyna. Now, a partial wall made of bricks and drywall stood nearly complete, partitioning off what used to be the playroom. There was just enough room for us to walk in the makeshift room one at a time, remaining connected by our hands. Raymond lifted his head and gasped at the same time as we did when we all saw what lay beyond the wall.

"A binding ceremony," Dr. Pike exclaimed. A white circle of salt had been spilled in the middle of the room. Black candles sputtered light and shadows around.

"Place him in the circle," Reyna directed. She walked over to a small table in the room and picked up more salt. Gabriel rolled the chair into the center of the circle and stepped over the salt on his way out. Reyna sprinkled more salt to cover where the chair had damaged the circle. "We need this to go well. Right, Daddy?"

"What is a binding ceremony?" I whispered with a tremble in my voice. I was scared Reyna would hear me but reminded myself that this was the past and she wasn't here. Reyna was somewhere in the present.

Reyna walked back to the table and picked up a herb. "Morning glory!" I called out, nearly pulling Brena and Teddy's hands from mine in excitement.

"It appears that she is binding Raymond to that circle. He will be, I mean would have been, unable to leave. Ever. He will remain in this circle without aging, his body held in the moment and time he was placed here," Dr. Pike explained.

"His biological processes won't function as normal. Meaning he won't need to eat, defecate, or urinate. He'll wither but still live for a very long time," Mom added.

"Is that living?" Loreen added with shock in her voice.

The entire group stood holding our breath as we watched Reyna walk over the circle and give a small cut to Raymond's palm. She collected drops of his blood in the morning glory. She walked over to the table and picked up a small cloth doll. It was a curious doll dressed in formal business wear of Ibeji Village with what appeared to be some hair on top.

"That's his poppet!" Dr. Pike advised. "She's going to use his blood on the doll to bind him to the circle."

"Maybe we've seen enough." Loreen poked her head in front of the group, trying to get anyone's attention. The rest of us focused on Reyna as she poured the blood on the doll and whispered her spell. She took the morning glory and loudly proclaimed, "I bind you, Raymond Yardley, to this circle. I bind you, Raymond Yardley, from your magic. I bind you, Raymond Yardley, from harming others or yourself. I bind you, Raymond Yardley, to this circle."

Raymond groaned. I looked over at Gabriel, who was standing back near the partial wall, his hands clasped in front of him and his head slightly hanging. His face was streaked with tears. I noticed more building materials behind him. "Do you think she's going to bind him and leave him in the cellar?" I asked the group. Dr. Pike nodded quietly while keeping her eyes on Reyna. I was the only one who noticed the nod. The rest were also focused on the young girl who had so much power. They already knew the answer anyway.

"Is she urinating?" Loreen asked as a clear liquid pooled around Reyna's feet from under her skirt.

"The baby!" Mom and Gabriel called out in unison.

"Don't worry about me!" Reyna shouted. "I'm done here. Finish the wall." She walked beyond the partial wall, past all of us, and towards the stairs.

We watched as Gabriel added more bricks to the open floor where the wall remained unsealed. A clang reverberated in the room as he accidentally dropped the brick trowel. A loud knock in the present brought us back into the present, around the kitchen table. The candles had nearly burned all the way down. A red bird flew down the hall and landed on the arm of the couch.

42

The knock at the door sounded again. Adu's head twisted between the bird on the couch and the door. She stood at attention with a low growl, the hair on her back standing straight up. I fought the urge to yell out something about someone knocking at the door like they were the police. "We have to get to the cellar. Raymond is down there," I directed.

"Wait." Mom got up to answer the door, side eyeing the bird. "It won't be that simple. Let me get rid of whoever this is and we can make a plan." She patted the dog to calm her.

At the door stood a much older Gabriel. The bird flew to his shoulder and rested there. Gabriel's once huge black afro was now tapered gray hair cut low with faded sides. His face and body were wrapped in weariness. But his eyes grew large and bright when he saw his sister facing him.

"Sis! Ba wo ni?" He walked in and hugged her tightly, her head pushed against his chest. She wrapped her arms around him just as tightly. I stood, scraping my chair across the kitchen floor when I realized who was at the door. The sound of the chair drove the bird to perch on a windowsill in the hallway.

The siblings let go and met each other's eyes as they held each other's hands. "I'm sorry to bust in like this," Gabriel started. "But you are all in danger. Reyna's here."

Mom let go of her brother's hand and turned to face me. I had already made my way to meet him. Gabriel followed his sister's look. He recognized me instantly.

"Ruby," he whispered, walking towards me.

I wasn't used to that name. I was breathless but managed to reply, "Imani."

Gabriel swept me up and hugged me. I was okay with it and hugged him back.

"I have been waiting so long to tell you how proud I am of you. You're so beautiful. You really are the spitting image of your mother." He turned to Mom then back to me. "Birth mother," he corrected, identifying the look of hurt that crossed his sister's face. "I didn't think it would take me this long to get back to you. I mean, back to where I could actually interact with you."

I let my dad go and watched him, unable to speak. I compared him to the pictures I had seen of him as a little boy. A stranger but still family. I shook my head, fighting the heaviness in my stomach.

"I'm so sorry for leaving you," Gabriel continued. "I didn't know if I would ever have the courage to face Reyna if she came for me. I left you with Brena to keep you safe. I thought it was the only way. But I didn't, did I? I didn't keep you safe." He dropped his head in the same way I had seen during the scrying vision only moments ago.

He leaned in, speaking more softly to me. "I wanted to warn you about Rome. I saw who he was from the beginning. But, if I got involved, I could have led Reyna to you. I couldn't take that chance. I didn't know if she was watching. I'm so sorry, baby girl. I should have been there."

I looked back towards Loreen and Teddy to see if they could hear. Teddy immediately looked up at the ceiling and Loreen turned to look around the kitchen. Dr. Pike stared intently at the whole scene. I turned back to my father. "The bird. Your red bird," I said.

"His name is Enitinwo." Gabriel nodded. "We've been watching you for a long time. In Chicago, I used spells and scrying to keep track of you. Here, Enitinwo has been doing most of the watching. When you two came back to Tiwa, to Ibeji Village, to this building," he waved his hand around, "I wanted to warn you. I knew she was close. But then I realized that you were the only one who could- who would- help your grandfather."

Gabriel craned his head around me to look at Loreen and Teddy. The bird mirrored his actions high on its perch. "You two met Reyna yesterday. She lives in the apartment that used to be her room."

"The old lady!" Teddy and Loreen said jointly, a bit of their memories coming back.

"Yes," Gabriel confirmed. "Going into her apartment alone was very dangerous. What happened in there? I left to find Imani after I saw you two go in."

"You met Reyna?" I asked, shocked.

Teddy and Loreen took a moment to try to recollect. "I still don't remember exactly what happened," Loreen answered.

"Me neither," Teddy added. They shared a confused look with each other then returned their attention to Gabriel. I felt a tug in my heart as it hit me that they kept pushing aside their own feelings to help me work through all this. I was glad I opened up to them. Figuring everything out meant I would be helping them, too.

"I'm sure Reyna has been watching what's going on in the building and using magic on this apartment," Gabriel interrupted my thoughts. "She probably used her magic on you two to find out how much you knew. It's a good thing you didn't know it was her or you wouldn't have made it out of there alive."

"She would have killed me?" Loreen exclaimed, clutching her chest. She stumbled back a couple of steps. Teddy leaned in and grabbed her around her shoulders, pulling her close to him with a quick squeeze before letting her go. She stayed close to him. I felt a twinge in my stomach.

"We do have to help Raymond," Teddy said. "I don't know why Reyna did what she did, but we can't leave him down there."

"No. That wouldn't be right. We do need to help him," Loreen said quietly. Her hand still rested on her chest. She leaned in closer to

Teddy. I fought the feeling in me that wanted them to move apart- just a little bit.

"You're right. I should have helped him back then." Gabriel looked back to the ground for a moment. The bird flew down and rested on his shoulder. Gabriel glanced from the bird to the group in front of him. "I have to make this right." He looked at me. "We'll have to face Reyna first or we'll never be able to help Raymond."

I turned towards everyone. "I have to face Reyna," I announced. "I'm the only one that can do it."

No one spoke. Dr. Pike studied me quietly. Teddy and Loreen watched me with awe. Gabriel opened his mouth to speak, a look of concern on his face. Enitinwo cocked his head at me.

Mom stepped next to me and hugged me close to her. "We have to prepare her."

43

"Magic in Tiwa draws on the person, on the nature around us, and on the community," Mom started, guiding me to the couch and encouraging me to take a seat. "You will need all of it to be able to face Reyna. She is lost and her magic is dark. Her being your mother," she paused as her voice cracked on the words 'your mother', "may not change how she deals with you."

I nodded. "I know, Mom. I have to be the one to face Reyna. I'm the one she's been targeting and she's already made you sick. I don't want anyone else to get hurt. Who knows what she would do if anyone else confronted her?" Members of the group either nodded in agreement or shrugged in response to my hypothetical question as they joined us in the living room. I didn't know if I was actually right; they were scared, or both.

"Our first form of defense has to be protection," Dr. Pike said. "We have to make sure before anything that you are protected through spells and objects."

"I'll keep this silk pouch on me. What else do you suggest?"

"Loreen, I'm aware that you keep a good protection spell on hand. With Brena's permission, see if you can find what you need," Dr. Pike directed.

"Yes, find what you need. You can start in the kitchen," Mom acknowledged.

"Ok. I'll be right back," Loreen said, heading into the kitchen.

"I also have the morning glory herb. Can I use that?" I asked.

Dr. Pike put her hand to her chin, thinking. She remained silent for so long, everyone grew worried.

"Dr. Pike?" Teddy called out.

"Yes, yes. I do think the morning glory will be helpful, but its use comes at a cost," she replied, looking at me.

"A cost?"

"You could use it to bind Reyna and stop her from using her magic. But using the morning glory the same way Reyna did with her father can darken your magic and, in the future, the intentions you set will be dark from the onset." Dr. Pike sat quietly again. "Possibly," she finished.

I thought for a moment. "It's also used for attracting things to you. Could there be a way for me to use it like that?"

"Interesting," Gabriel spoke up. "Since she's your mother, you could use an attraction spell as a form of protection. That could make sure you remain safe."

"Then what?" Mom cried. "She doesn't hurt Imani, but what about Raymond? What about us?"

"We'll go with her, sis," Gabriel responded. "Between the three of us, we can find a way to bind her without risking Imani's safety or magic."

"Here." Loreen stood in front of me holding a dark bottle of liquid.

"What's this?" I asked, taking the bottle from her.

"It's an uncrossing bath."

"Genius!" Dr. Pike exclaimed, startling everyone. Loreen smiled widely. "An uncrossing bath is usually used to break cords. Their connections to people. But I added some of the morning glory to it as well. It will break Reyna's cord connection to Imani and Raymond and bind her magic as well!" Dr. Pike stood from the couch in her excitement. "Angel, you have far exceeded my expectations. I feel like you should get an A in my course just from your sheer brilliance in solving this matter."

"It was Imani who inspired me," Loreen said, sitting in the space between me and Teddy on the couch. "If she hadn't gotten the morning glory in the first place, it would have never occurred to me."

Teddy watched Loreen. He looked impressed with her new ability to give someone else, especially me, credit. I silently agreed.

"Ok, baby girl. We'll go with you," Mom confirmed.

"And we," Dr. Pike said, motioning towards Loreen and Teddy, "will go to the basement and start breaking down that wall to find Raymond. Come on Teddy, let's see if we can earn you an 'A' as well."

44

I remembered the last time I had stood in front of apartment 8B, against my will and unable to move. Dread set in. I fidgeted with the orange, furry, plush ball that was attached to my bag. Mom touched my shoulder softly. "It's okay, baby girl. We're here with you."

"Enitinwo is outside the apartment. He'll see us through the window," Gabriel reminded me. "He can get your friends if we need them." Despite their reassurances, I still jumped a little when he knocked on the door.

"Just a moment!" a woman's voice called out. The door opened shortly to reveal not an old woman who would have struggled to carry packages up a single flight of stairs- as Teddy and Loreen had described her- but a woman in her late 30s. Her right index finger had a silver serpent ring with a single bluish green eye. If the woman would have worn long braids instead of a colorful head wrap, she would have been my spitting image. And yet, I recognized her as a younger version of...

"Ellie," I whispered. I stepped back as I noticed the same crescent-shaped eyes and short wide nose on the woman's face that I'd had dinner with a few nights ago. Tracing the contours of her face that resembled my own, I hadn't noticed then that it was the same eyes and nose that I'd seen so many times in the mirror. For a moment, I lost my purpose. I'd forgotten the reasons I stood in front of this woman who was my mother. How could this woman, my mother, who had given birth to me, who I just cooked with and who comforted me when I was feeling scared and lonely, be the source of so much darkness? The connection

I thought I had shattered under the weight of confusion and suspicion. Another squeeze from Mom again brought me back to the present.

Reyna, taller than Mom but shorter than Gabriel, took her time while examining us from head to toe. She gave Gabriel a stern look, a soft one to me, and smiled at Mom. She looked at each of us an equal amount of time, as if none of us deserved extra attention. Not even the daughter she'd given birth.

"Can't say I haven't been expecting you," she said, a lingering smile playing on her lips. "Would you like to come in?"

Stepping aside, she gestured for us to enter, inviting us into her domain. As I crossed the threshold, my eyes searched for the familiar presence of Ellie, the one who had aided me just days ago. Yet, all I found was Reyna, a woman who seemed motivated solely by her own interests.

45

The smell of compost gently wafted around Teddy, Loreen, and Dr. Pike. "Behind those bins," Teddy pointed out. Having just left the room as it was nearly twenty years ago, it was easy to see where the wall had been placed. Teddy noted to himself he would have never seen the new wall if he hadn't participated in the scrying. The addition blended seamlessly. The effort Gabriel put in some twenty years ago was probably why it was missed during the renovation. Teddy walked over and pushed the bins to the sides opening more space to work.

Dr. Pike's bag clanged with a thud after she dropped it onto the floor. "I'm glad I was over-prepared," she said, opening the bag, reaching in, and pulling out a chisel and a sledgehammer.

"Over prepared?" Loreen sung. "Who thinks to have a chisel and sledgehammer on them?" She peeped incredulously at all the other tools poking out of the professor's bag.

"I am a historian, young lady," Dr. Pike said. She handed tools and safety goggles to Teddy. "As a historian," she continued and handed Loreen safety goggles, "I must be ready to find artifacts wherever they are. These are the tools I usually bring with me. Did I ever tell you students about my travels to Ina Village, where I found the Spear of Idagba? Well, as it was, I was with my research students and on this particular day, we hadn't found anything in our excavations. It was-"

"Dr. Pike, can you give me a hand with this?" Teddy interrupted. In his left hand, he held pieces of drywall he managed to loosen. The hammer hung limply in his right. "I'm trying to remove pieces of the wall as I get them loose."

"Yes, yes. Magic isn't going to knock this wall down tonight. Let's get started." Dr. Pike carried her bag closer to where Teddy was working.

Teddy smashed through the drywall with ease. "I'm at the bricks in this section. I'm going to see how loose they are. If I can get some out the way." Dr. Pike handed him a crowbar.

Teddy grunted, edged out some of the grout, and heaved out three bricks, enough to see beyond the wall. "I can't see anything," he said, peering through the darkness. "Do you happen to have a flashlight, Dr. Pike?"

"As my great grandfather used to say, it is the person in a hurry who studies the complexion of the day," Dr. Pike said, finding the flashlight in her bag. Teddy and Loreen exchanged a look, making Loreen giggle.

The flashlight cut the darkness into small slices. Teddy oscillated it methodically to the right and up and down. He hesitated near the center of the room and found the wheels of a rolling chair. Scanning over, he saw two brown feet. He lifted the light higher and saw the withered version of Raymond Yardley tied to the chair. Raymond's head was hanging and he appeared much more emaciated than the group had seen in their vision upstairs.

Teddy jumped back and away from the hole. "I see him. I see Raymond," he spoke softly. He tried to shake the sight of Raymond's nearly skin and bones appearance out of his head.

"It's too high, Teddy," Loreen said, scanning the room for a stool or chair.

"It appears you've made the hole at your eye level, Teddy. Tell us what you see," Dr. Pike advised. Teddy sighed before using the light to search back where he'd found Raymond. He identified a thin white line surrounding him. "I see the salt circle." Teddy shined the light directly onto Raymond's face. The elderly man's eyes, jaundiced and sitting visibly in the socket, held Teddy's gaze captive.

"Help me." Raymond's voice was hoarse and his mouth barely moved. "Help me."

"We're going to help. We'll be right there," Teddy said kindly. He turned to the women. "We have some work to do."

46

We entered the apartment, moving in unison, our walks jaunty, our posture stiff and unnatural. Reyna's apartment was nearly as green as the shopkeeper's. Various plants and cuttings hung on floating shelves throughout the living room. Colorful pots and planters held large ferns and small indoor trees. The size of the apartment was comparable to mine but the layout was very different. The living room and kitchen were not as open. Instead, they were divided by a wall that had an opening cut out over the stove. This must've been where she really stayed. The apartment she used as "Ellie" didn't appear nearly as lived in.

"I see you've finally brought my child to me, Gabriel." Reyna's voice was sweet but filled with all the tenderness a bear has for its food. I tried to search for traces of the woman I'd spent time with the other night. Reyna sat comfortably in an armchair across from us on the couch. I couldn't help but be reminded of meeting my grandmother, Selene- Mom and Gabriel's mother- the day before in a similar manner. Now I faced my own.

"You left us," Gabriel responded matter-of-factly. He sat on the edge of the couch, between Mom and me. He leaned in front of us, in a protective position.

"You didn't have to hide her from me, Gabriel. I mean, I came back and you were gone." She met her former lover with nonchalance.

Gabriel let out a puff of air. "You left me with a three-month-old without any word. I didn't know what happened to you."

Reyna got up and walked into the kitchen. Our heads moved as one as we peered through the opening above the stove while Reyna prepared a kettle of water. She smiled graciously at us, as if it really was a nice family visit. It was still kind of dawning on me that it was a family visit, just not the kind most people had. Trying to save the trapped grandfather from the mother they knew she was keeping captive.

"Would anyone like tea?" Reyna asked, interrupting the cacophony of thoughts in my head.

I sat, stunned. I was still working on accepting what my newly identified family looked like. I felt like an observer of the events, seeing everything outside of myself. Mom and Gabriel looked at each other with anxious tinges. Reyna came back into the room with a tray holding a mug, a jar of honey, and a couple bags of tea. The slight slam of the tray on the wooden table next to her chair jolted me back into my body.

"I know you probably would have enjoyed your job working in the gardens, Ms. Brena," Reyna said, focused on stirring the honey into her tea. "That's what you did before you left Tiwa, right? It's a shame you got sick before you could even start."

"You?" Mom exclaimed.

"Pst." Reyna sucked her teeth. She blew on a spoonful of tea, maintaining eye contact with my mother. My aunt? "I made you sick so I could better watch over Imani."

Reyna had been watching over me. That made sense. Running into Ellie at the bookstore right after seeing the monstrous version of myself in the mirror. But, she made Mom sick? She did the haunting?

Gabriel held Mom's hand, stopping her from moving out of her seat. He whispered to her, reminding her of what we were there to accomplish.

Reyna's cold gaze turned on me. "I did my best to encourage you to leave young lady."

I felt a tiny tingle of warmth that soon turned into a chill down my spine. She was haunting me. The evil mirror version of me. The chairs trying to attack me. The shower sludge. It had been Reyna. How could a mother treat her daughter like that? Reyna smiled. I was reminded of her younger self, before her father broke her heart. I wondered if she could see the brokenness in me, too. Her face was a blank slate, unreadable, as she sipped her tea.

"What do you want from them, Reyna?" Gabriel asked.

"I didn't even know she was still alive, Gabriel," she spat out. "As soon as I saw her, I knew she was mine. She's my daughter, Gabriel. You took her. You hid her." Her voice was agitated, angry. Her body remained calm.

"But she awakened Raymond with her presence," she continued. "He's been calling her. I don't know how he still has the strength or how he knows she's here; he knows she can free him."

The low tone of her voice was scary. I had no idea what dark things she could be capable of with us just feet away from her. I fingered the jar in my bag. Its touch- its purpose- helped to calm my nerves. Mom's gaze bore into me; I met and followed her glance to the shelf on the wall behind and to the left of Reyna. A small doll that looked just like Reyna peeked from behind one of the plants on the shelf. I looked back at Mom with wide eyes. A poppet doll.

"We're not here to fight, Reyna. We just want to help Raymond." Gabriel spoke evenly when he mentioned her father's name.

Reyna placed her tea down on the table slowly. She placed her hands in her lap and stared at Gabriel. "My father cannot be helped," she said monotonously.

Without warning, she was rushing towards him. Gabriel tried to stand before she reached him but found himself falling back and Reyna grabbing his face. I flew out of my seat, ran to the shelf, and grabbed the doll. I took a pair of scissors from the shelf below it. Mom moved to get Reyna off her brother, yanking at her shoulder. Reyna stood and pushed Mom off her with ease. The odd smile returned to her face. She watched in silence as Mom bent down to help Gabriel. There was a collection of tiny herbs stuck to Gabriel's face.

"I...I can't move, sis." His body sat frozen, propped up against the couch, his legs stretched towards Reyna. Mom snatched a cloth off Reyna's tray, her eyes filled with both concern and fury. With determined hands, she attempted to wipe the stubborn herbs that clung to Gabriel's face, hoping to restore his mobility.

Time stood still as Mom's touch met Gabriel's skin, but the herbs resisted her efforts. It was as if Reyna's dark influence had penetrated every fiber of Gabriel's being, rendering him helpless, and leaving us on the edge of despair.

Reyna watched, her satisfaction palpable, reveling in the chaos she had caused. Her eyes gleamed with a twisted pleasure, relishing the power she held over us.

"Reyna!" I called out, distracting the woman from the scene. She turned her sinister look towards me as I moved in closer. Her overconfidence would be her downfall. I threw the bath Loreen had prepared on Reyna's face. She screamed as she threw her body at me. The bath penetrated her darkness. She stopped nearly midair- just as she was about to reach me.

"What did you do?" Reyna cried out, her hands trying to wipe the bath off her face. The scent of morning glory in the concoction- now a sweeter essence than what I'd been smelling in the building- wafted towards me as I strutted up to her. I pulled the wrap off her head and used the scissors to cut a lock of her hair.

47

Loreen, Teddy, and Dr. Pike stood behind the narrow opening Teddy had completed. They surveyed the room with their flashlights and trails of light from the basement shined in. "Be sure not to cross the circle," Dr. Pike warned. "Once a spell has been executed, the circle becomes sacred. You don't want to risk becoming part of the spell."

"I don't see anything over here we can use," Teddy called out. He stood by the table containing leftover candle wax from the candles Reyna had burned nearly twenty years ago when she imprisoned her father. Other remnants of her magic sat on the table covered by dust and cobwebs.

"He doesn't look good," Loreen informed the group. She used her flashlight to check Raymond as well as she could from a distance. His veins were visible through his nearly paper-thin skin. They held their breath politely at the smell of decay that exuded from him. Loreen moved the light to his head, which was once again lowered on his chest.

Raymond snapped his head up. Loreen took a large step back, surprised by the movement. Shocked by his gaunt face and bulging eyes, she lowered the light to the ground.

"Release me," Raymond whispered hoarsely.

"We need to at least get him some water," Teddy said, now standing next to Loreen and Dr. Pike, observing the man.

"Release me. I want to go." Raymond's voice grew in strength. His body shifted slightly in the chair. "My time to go has passed. I want to go."

"I don't do a lot of blood magic. I'm not sure how to reverse that spell," Dr. Pike replied.

"My descendants." Raymond was now nearly sitting upright in the chair. The trio could see the shadow of the man he used to be. Pity pierced their hearts. "They're close. My descendants are here. I've felt them in this building. I've been trying to contact them."

"Do you mean Imani?" Teddy's voice went up an octave as he connected what was going on.

"I've been using what energy and magic I've had to contact them. I can feel them. They can help me."

"He's been doing the strange things to Imani in the apartment," Loreen gasped. "The visions, the sounds, the sights. It even makes sense that he was doing the possessions. Leading Imani to Reyna, letting her know he was here as well."

"Hmm...yes. I see," Dr. Pike said thoughtfully. "It does explain some of the events, but not all of them. What about her mother's illness? And the dark mirror version of her."

The group was quiet. Raymond moaned.

"I don't know," Loreen said. "But either Reyna or Imani have to help him. And I don't think Reyna is going to do it."

"I'll go get Imani," Teddy said. "You two stay here with him. Get him some water, if you can. I'm going to the apartment to get her. Adu, come."

<h1 style="text-align:center">48</h1>

Reyna screamed in anguish as liquid, herbs, and morning glory dripped down the length of her body. My fingers fumbled with the pins. I worked quickly to stick Reyna's hair to the poppet before she had a chance to recover. Once the hair was in place, I pulled a vine of morning glory from my bag and began wrapping it around the doll. I envisioned Reyna as the little girl I had first encountered in the basement, running playfully with her mother. A little girl full of joy, enjoying playtime with her mother. Then I remembered the teen who bound her father in perpetuity. A monster who used blood magic to get her revenge. I imagined each wind of the morning glory binding the woman's dark power.

Reyna's hand darted to the concealed pocket in her skirt. Emitting an incoherent cry, she clumsily charged at me, brandishing a handful of herbs. Swiftly sidestepping her attack, I narrowly evaded her grasp. In her unbalanced state, Reyna careened into the wall behind me, toppling a shelf laden with verdant foliage in the process.

I closed my eyes. I took a brief breath to say a quiet prayer to my ancestors. "I bind you, Reyna Yardley, from using your magic to harm others," I chanted out loud, continuing to wind the vine around the poppet. "I bind you, Reyna Yardley, from using magic for personal gain. I bind you, Reyna Yardley, from using magic to undo your pain."

Reyna groaned from her seated position against the wall. Her groan abated into a long continuous cry. I tied the last bit of vine onto itself.

Her cry quieted into small, sorrowful wails. I placed the doll in my bag and ran over to check on my father.

"Are you okay?" I asked as I sat at Gabriel's side.

"I think the binding worked," he replied. "I can feel something in my toes."

"I can't believe you did that, Imani. You learned so much in my absence." Mom hugged me with one arm.

Reyna graduated from tears and sobs to actual words. "What would you do? What would you do if he killed your mother slowly? Not with a knife or a weapon. But by withdrawing his love. By taking away his care." Her chest heaved in disordered bursts, until she was absolutely still- bound by the poppet, entrenched in her suffering.

Mom and I met each other's glances with the same look of pity. Yardley Place no longer elicited fear and confusion for me. Understanding the root of my family's pain- the war Reyna felt due to a mother's love gone and dead because of a father's detachment- brought me clarity.

A knock at the door jostled me out of my thoughts. I opened it and let Teddy and Adu in.

After a quick survey of the scene, Adu immediately went over to Reyna to guard her and Teddy turned towards me. My face said everything he needed to know. "He needs you, Imani. It has to be his descendant that frees him," he finally said.

I nodded.

"Wait just a moment," Mom called out. She examined each of the plants in the room. One near the kitchen in a pot patterned with bright geometric shapes was of particular interest. Another hoisted above Reyna's sitting position caused her to sigh hopefully.

"Scissors," she said, reaching out her hand.

"What are they for?" I asked, giving them to her.

"This one," she answered, snipping the one near the kitchen window, "is for my brother. It'll speed his recovery." Teddy and I watched as she slipped into the kitchen and poured the rest of Reyna's hot water over the herb. She sat the new cup of tea on the tray where Reyna's cup sat. She took Reyna's teacup and placed it back into the kitchen. "Give it a few moments to seep, Gabriel," she advised, placing the tray next to Gabriel's head on the couch.

"This one is for you, baby girl." She stood next to Reyna who was silently sobbing and cut a stem and leaves from the plant above her. "Put this in your bag. When you get to Raymond-"

"Go with them, Brena," Gabriel instructed. "I'll be fine here with the dog and Reyna."

Mom eyed Reyna. Reyna held her face behind her hands, still weeping. Adu looked at Mom and gently nodded. Bound from her powers, all Reyna had left were the emotions she'd denied herself. All she had left was her pain.

"Ok. We'll be back as soon as we're done," Mom sighed. She motioned to Teddy and me to go.

Gabriel nodded and turned his head towards the tea, trying to lap it like a kitten.

49

I gasped. My grandfather's withered and dried up version of his former self had no remnants of the stature he used to have. While I understood Reyna's pain, I could not justify this treatment, this type of vengeance on anyone.

Not even Rome? I wondered to myself, grateful the thought of my former friend didn't debilitate me. Instead, hope in healing energized me. I knew that I could heal and didn't have to be as vindictive as my birth mother.

"What do we need to do?" I asked, looking at Mom.

"Bring the herbs I got from Reyna's apartment to this table," she commanded. "Teddy, bring me that chisel."

We did as we were told. Mom grinded the herbs and stems into tiny pieces with the head of the chisel. "Help me sprinkle this on the salt," she said to no one in particular.

Loreen, Teddy, and I swept the ground herbs from the table into our hands. Loreen crouched, took pieces out of her hand, and carefully sprinkled it onto the salt. Teddy squatted and squeezed the pieces out of his closed fist into a tiny line on the salt. I bent over and sprinkled the other third of the salt circle, moving slowly and carefully.

"Now what?" Loreen inquired.

"The poppet. We have to find his poppet," Dr. Pike advised.

Flashlights cut through the darkness of the impromptu room. We tried to find hiding spots tight enough to fit the doll. Teddy craned his fingers into what appeared to be a crack in the original wall of the room. He tried to pry the crack open with his fingers, but learned it was just a crack.

Loreen moved the table out of the way and inspected the entire floor and wall it covered. Unable to find any potential hiding spots, she moved down to another section of the wall. "How do we know the poppet is down here? What if it's in her apartment?" she asked, her flashlight scanning the wall and floor.

"It's usually kept close enough to the intended so it can maintain its power," Dr. Pike replied. She was squatting on the other side of the room, looking for a hiding spot. She stood and faced the sound of Loreen's voice. "However, Reyna may have kept it with her all these years. To ensure no one could help her father." She placed a hand on her hips and breathed out strongly. "Hmph," she muttered.

I found a tiny vent at the bottom of the wall, close to a corner. I peered into it with my flashlight and saw something small reflecting back in the light. "I think I found something. I need help to get these screws out."

Dr. Pike went and searched inside her bag of tools. The clang vibrated throughout the room. "Here you are," she said, holding out the screwdriver to me. "And here are some different heads if you need them."

Teddy grabbed the screwdriver and set of heads from the professor and walked over to where I remained crouching. "I got it," he said, bending next to me and examining the screws. I stood and backed up, watching him fit the right size head and start extracting the screws. He removed the grate and reached in, stretching as far as his shoulder into the opening. "I can't reach it," he grimaced.

"We can." Loreen pulled Iranran from her shirt pocket.

"You had that with you?" I whispered.

"Most times." Loreen nuzzled her gecko's nose then gently placed it inside the vent's opening. Within moments, the gecko's head emerged, clinging onto a doll with its feet. Loreen gathered the doll in one hand and placed Iranran back in her pocket. She examined the poppet with her flashlight.

Raymond's blood and morning glory enveloped the doll, as Reyna had left it twenty years ago. The plant was still nearly intact, just as Raymond was. "This is it," she announced.

50

⬦

Reyna remained on the floor by the wall, muted. She looked at Adu then immediately away. She examined the space around her. Her home had a new meaning without the use of her magic to harm others. The anger she would have felt yesterday was repose in this moment. She felt different in her body, lighter. She contemplated the purpose of her magic. Its uses beyond harming others. Beyond vengeance. Beyond fear. She'd almost contemplated her own purpose, but instead welcomed Gabriel's interruption.

"I'm glad you got to see her," Gabriel said. He'd nearly finished the tea and held the cup midair. He sat calmly on the couch, as if he'd already forgotten the altercation between him and his former lover. "She looks so much like you, but personality wise, you two are very different."

"She's been here for such a little time and she made good use of that time. She's clever," Reyna said. She lifted herself from the floor. "May I?" she asked Adu, pointing to the chair that was closer to Gabriel. Adu got behind Reyna and herded her to the chair. Gabriel stared at Reyna's apron with the secret pocket. They looked at each other, both aware that she could no longer use the hidden herbs for harm. She removed the apron and placed it on the couch near Gabriel.

"You've been here this whole time?" Gabriel asked, smiling slightly.

Reyna shook her head. "You know, I remember watching you and Ruby sleep when I left. You held her on your chest and her tiny body was sprawled out. She had this cute little tiny snore." Reyna smiled as she traveled back in her memory. "I knew I couldn't stay here with him

190

down in the cellar. I told myself I had to finalize his business affairs. Make sure no one would come looking for him or ask any questions." She looked directly at Gabriel. "And I didn't need you for that anymore. I really didn't see how she could fit into my life. After I bound him, I felt more connected to him. I had become more like him and less like my mother. Ruby needed someone like my mother. I didn't realize that by trapping him down there, I'd be trapping myself. So, I left for the Oke Mountains.

"I stayed there for a while. Alone. I made sure the last remaining property, Yardley Place, was mine by putting it into a trust that no one could trace back to me. I needed to be sure that no one found him. After a while, the building started calling me back. He was calling me back."

Gabriel leaned forward, drawn in by the details he'd waited twenty years to hear.

"I couldn't risk being noticed, so I maintained a glamor spell to look like an old woman. Some time ago, I tried searching for you. I used everything I could to find you and Ruby. Divination, scrying, a private investigator," Reyna chuckled. "The water that one is destined to drink will never flow past one. When I saw that young lady walk into Yardley Place, my spitting image, I knew it was Ruby. All my efforts and she just showed up. Then, when I realized that you left her, too, with your sister, I was angry.

"I should have been angry at myself. But I was angry at you, at your sister, and at Ruby. For all the things that I let get in my own way, they had pushed back and thrived against their own struggles. It made me so mad." Reyna leaned down in the chair, tears falling from her eyes again.

Gabriel watched her. He was reminded of the little girl who had been stuck in her room reading books all day. The little girl he had escorted from the dinner party who only wanted to play the game. To be loved by her father.

"You have been angry a long time, Reyna. I know your father put you and your mother through a lot. But I never agreed with what you did to him. You took everything from him. And you coerced me into doing it with you. I felt so helpless at the time." Gabriel gulped down his shame. "I will always regret helping you."

"He was evil, Gabriel," Reyna's voice cracked. "You saw how my mother died. He broke her heart. In the process, he broke me."

"Your pain was so heavy, Reyna. I felt it every day in this house. It's partly why I stayed with you. But the answer wasn't revenge. You were so isolated. I've been wondering for years how it all would have turned out if I'd gotten a Counselor to help you. You needed a professional to talk to. You needed community. Instead of using your magic to bind your father, you could have used it to heal. Along with therapy. I should have helped you in a better way. Not the way you wanted. But the way you needed."

Reyna sat. She remembered what it had been like to have hope. To believe that someone would save her from her father's emotional abuse. She could almost pinpoint that moment when she realized she was stuck and no one was coming. Not even Gabriel could have saved her from herself then. All she had was her revenge, her darkness, and her magic.

"Oh my goodness," she breathed. "I did the same thing to Ruby. I mean Imani. I terrorized her and left her alone and hopeless."

The fog of regret, shame, and suffering condensed around the former couple. They locked eyes in the stillness, stifling the deeds of the past that could not be undone and acknowledging the positive outcome: Imani.

"Brena did a good job raising our daughter," Gabriel stated plainly, finally breaking the silence. "I don't know that I'd do that well with Ruby on my own. Any darkness that Ruby would've inherited from you and Raymond was drowned out by Brena's love. Plus, she had therapy on the mainland. She's built her resilience. Imagine if you'd had therapy after your mother died. Your magic would not be so dark. You would not have been alone."

Reyna released an audible gasp before allowing the comfort of silence to return.

"She really didn't know about me?" Reyna's voice was soft.

"She didn't know about either of us. I made Brena promise not to tell her anything. I didn't even tell Brena about you, just to be sure." Gabriel sat up straighter. He flexed his legs. "I watched her though. She's a good kid. I think there was a time when she felt lonely. Her best friend moved away. She let the wrong person fill that void." He looked down at his hands. "I think she's moving past that now. I don't know. I hope so."

"Loneliness can do so many things to you," Reyna replied. Gabriel nodded, understanding that she was talking about herself. "I have to fix my own mistakes, Gabriel. I can't let her do it." Her voice was full of conviction. She stood from the chair. Adu growled softly. "I really want to help. Will you let me help?"

Adu looked to Gabriel. Gabriel stood with confidence and gently grabbed the mother of his child's hand. He covered her hand with his other hand and held it a little longer, looking directly into Reyna's face. "You're bound, Reyna. You won't be able to do any harm."

Reyna nodded and slowly pulled her hand back to her side. "Let's go help our daughter. Let's go help my father."

Adu barked.

51

"I don't want to do blood magic," I said. I held the poppet and turned it around in my hands, examining it for the answers I needed. "I don't think I even fully understand the consequences. I just know it'll be bad."

Dr. Pike studied the doll from afar. Mom watched me trying to figure things out. Neither were stepping in. I think they both understood that I needed to lead. I needed to determine what path we would take in freeing Raymond.

"What if we just did it in reverse?" Loreen offered. Everyone looked at her.

"That's too much like right," Teddy laughed.

"That is an excellent idea, my dear," Dr. Pike added.

"Yea." I tilted my head to the side, looking at the doll. "Can we do that?"

"That's definitely part of it," Mom said. "But-"

"But, you'll need to use a cleansing bath as well," a voice from beyond the wall interjected. We turned around to see Reyna, followed by Gabriel and Adu, coming in through the opening. Mom immediately stepped in front of me, scowling at Reyna. Raymond moaned from his seat. Adu flopped down next to the table.

"I'm here to help." Reyna waved her hands in the air as if she were holding a white flag. Mom remained in position. Reyna walked towards her father and stood just outside the circle.

"It's okay, sis. She really is. Anyway, her magic's been bound by Ru-, I mean Imani."

"I'm going to help you, Dad," Reyna said to Raymond.

Mom regarded the woman and her actions. She listened to her brother's words and relaxed. But she didn't move.

"I brought some things to help," Reyna continued. She pulled out a jar full of herbs and fruit peels floating in a clear liquid, a jar of spices, and new candles. She placed them on the small table in the room, removing the older items. She turned to face the group. Teddy and Loreen exchanged a glance, each raising their eyebrows.

"What if those are the same things she used to drug us?" Loreen called out.

Reyna looked towards Loreen and Teddy. "I know I don't deserve your trust. I'm sorry that I put you in harm's way. I only want to make things right. Not just for my father, but for everyone." Her eyes pleaded in my direction. "Imani, will you help me?" Reyna asked.

I stepped from behind Mom, touching her shoulder. I moved next to Reyna. For a moment, I allowed myself to fully acknowledge that this was my mother. In that same moment, I saw pride exude from her face. Still looking at me, Reyna reached for the jar. "This is a cleansing bath. This will help him remove some of the magic. But we'll need to use it on the poppet until we can clear some of the magic from the circle. We can do this together." Reyna turned to her audience.

"Will one of you help me with the candles? And add this to the circle." She motioned with a bottle of spices and bag of white candles in her hand.

Teddy grabbed the spices and added it to the herbs already sprinkled on the circle. Loreen began lighting the candles. "Place them around the circle as you light them," Reyna commanded.

Dr. Pike went to stand closer to Mom. "Are we sure this is okay?" she asked her. "Can we trust her?"

"Imani bound her from using her magic to harm others. Either this is a ploy to stall for some reason or she is actually helping. What are your thoughts on the tools she's using?"

Dr. Pike studied the jar from afar. She walked over to Teddy and held out her hand to request a pinch of the herbs. She sniffed them, then placed it on the salt circle before going back to Brena.

"Looks like a cleansing bath and more rosemary. It seems she's adding the same herb that you had us add earlier," Dr. Pike informed Mom.

Mom nodded. "I think it's okay," she said.

"It is okay, sis." Mom jumped a bit as Gabriel stepped in and joined the conversation. "It'll be okay," he continued. I noticed for the first time that he held a broom in his hands.

With the candles lit and the salt nearly completely covered by rosemary, Reyna instructed us to form a circle around the salt. I stood next to her, holding Raymond's poppet. Reyna held the bath. "As Imani and I cleanse the doll, we all need to visualize Raymond being cleansed and unbound. Gabriel, will you start the chant?"

Gabriel closed his eyes as the words came from him musically, his voice holding a baritone timbre. "Though love was once sought, it is love we now seek. Break the binds meant for eternity." The rest of the group, minus Reyna and I, joined him in closing their eyes. Dr. Pike and Mom began swaying to the rhythm of the chant. Teddy used his hands on his chest to form an accompanying beat. Loreen swayed to the rhythm.

I held the poppet and Reyna slowly poured the bath on top of its head. I closed my eyes and envisioned the bath pouring down the head of my anguished grandfather, his body being cleansed of the blood magic Reyna had put into place on the day of my birth. I opened my eyes to look at Raymond and saw liquid dripping down his head. I saw strength start to return to his face and body as he sat up in the chair. Once the liquid was gone from the jar, Reyna turned to face her father.

"I'm sorry, Baba." Reyna kneeled down behind the salt circle and lowered her head to the ground. Raymond sat fully upright in the chair. His body was returning to the state it was in nearly twenty years ago, before he was imprisoned in the circle. We saw his stature even as he sat in the chair.

"Stand, Ododo. We both are responsible for what occurred between us, but I will take it all. I forgive you. We will work through this from the altar. Do what is next."

I stood before the full stature of my grandfather, Raymond, nearly released from the revenge spell my biological mother had cast upon him. I gazed at him, a mix of emotions swirling within me. I'd never known my grandfather and didn't understand the circumstances that led to Reyna's actions. Yet, I could feel the weight of the past, the unspoken pain and unresolved guilt that lingered in the room.

"Release me. I want to go," Raymond's voice broke through the stillness, carrying a plea for freedom tinged with resignation. His body shifted slightly, as if the silent longing for release emanated from the confines of his once frozen existence. "My time to go has passed. I want to go."

My heart ached with a newfound understanding. I had grown up with a loving mother- an aunt who loved me as her own. Who was my biological mother? What I now knew about my biological mother's tumultuous relationship with her father painted a picture of neglect, loss, and the profound impact it had on our family. In that moment, I realized that my grandfather's entrapment mirrored the emotional imprisonment he had subjected Reyna to, perpetuating a cycle of pain and revenge.

With trepidation, I took a step closer to my grandfather, my voice trembling as I spoke. "Grandpa Raymond, though I never knew you, I've seen the scars left ripple through our family. The consequences of your actions have shaped our lives and brought us to this point."

Raymond's eyes flickered, a spark of recognition dancing within them. As if he'd already played this scene over and over again in his mind. I watched as it became real to him, the realization of his own failings dawning on him, breaking through to the reality he now fully faced. A single tear escaped his eye, glistening like a diamond in the dim light.

I continued, my voice filled with compassion and a desire for healing. "It's time, Raymond. This is the moment to face the truth and acknowledge the pain. The neglect and loss inflicted upon my biological mother tore our family apart. We have carried the burden of that pain, but we also have the power to break free from it."

Raymond's voice carried through the room as he found his strength to speak, now fully recovered to his previous state. His words were laden with remorse and regret. "Imani, my dear granddaughter, though I failed as a father, I see now the depth of my neglect. The pain I caused your mother and the grief that followed...It's a burden that I've carried all this time for far too long.

"I failed her," he confessed, his voice choked with emotion. "I failed my daughter and her mother- my beautiful, sweet wife. My neglect, my selfishness...it poisoned the love that once bound us. I watched as their world crumbled, unable to break free from my own self-absorption. The pain they endured, the loss they suffered...it's a weight I can never undo."

Reyna was now standing, her face drenched in her tears. Raymond moved towards her as if to hug her but remembered the confines of the salt. He pulled back, closed his eyes and shook his head. Reyna clutched herself in a self-hug. I wrapped my arms around her shoulders.

"Now, in this moment of clarity," Raymond continued, making full eye contact with his daughter, "I see the consequences of my actions. I see the depth of your pain, daughter, the void left behind by your mother's absence. It is my responsibility, it has always been my responsibility, to acknowledge the role I played in your suffering."

He paused, his voice cracking with emotion. "I cannot undo the past, the years lost and the love withheld. But I am ready to confront my mistakes and seek forgiveness. I want to break free from this cycle that has haunted our family.

"I want to be free, not just from this spell, but from the shackles of my own shortcomings. I will face the truth, seek redemption, and honor the memory of the women I loved and lost. I need to find peace, not just for my own sake, but for the sake of my daughter's legacy."

As his words hung in the air, a profound silence filled the room. All of us, witnesses to his revelation, felt the weight of his remorse and the strength of his desire for release. In that moment, the collective resolve to set him free grew stronger, fueled by the understanding that true liberation came not only from breaking the spell but from his sincere self-realization and unwavering remorse.

Reyna straightened her shoulders and wiped away her tears. "Thank you, Baba," she whispered. She took the broom from Gabriel's hands and started sweeping the salt circle away. The others moved away as she neared them, making sure the broom did not cross their feet. Raymond stood and fixed his clothing, which was also now repaired to the same state as nearly twenty years ago. He turned to me and smiled softly.

"Do not let the sins of family become your curse. Do not let the sins of others become your burden. You are a Yardley. The strength is already within you."

I nodded as I watched dust whirl in a circle where his feet were placed. The dust extended upwards, coating his body until he was completely covered. Shortly, only dust billowed into a twirl that drifted to the ground as Reyna swept the last of the salt circle into a pile. There was no sign of the body that was in front of me moments ago. I pressed my palm to my heart and muttered a prayer under my breath. I inhaled with a gasp as the pile in front of the chair nearly disappeared completely. My grandfather was gone.

A shriek pulled my attention away from the last speck of dust disappearing. I turned to the source of the sound to see dust gathering at my birth mother's feet, rising and enveloping Reyna's entire body. Her silhouette could barely be seen as she the dust swarmed around her like a cloud of soundless gnats. I watched in horror as she disappeared from sight, trapped in the swirl of dust. "I'm sorry," Reyna's voiced gasped in her final breath to me before she was completely enshrouded. "Oh, baby girl." Mom pulled me close to her as the dust metamorphosed into a quickly disappearing pile. Reyna was gone. My mother was gone.

52

Friday

I rolled over, awakened by the crisp breeze coming through Mom's bedroom window. The sun kissed my forehead. Jasmine wafted in the air.

"Good morning, baby girl," Mom sat on the side of the bed, fully dressed. She lifted her head from the book she was reading.

"What time is it?" I asked groggily, wiping the sleep away.

"Nearly noon, but still morning," she smiled. She reached for a glass of water on her nightstand and offered it to me.

"Thank you." I sat up and gulped the drink down.

"How are you?"

"I'm up." I put the glass back.

"I mean, how are you?" she repeated. She put her book down and placed all of her attention on me.

"I don't know, Mom."

"Do you understand what happened?"

I shrugged. "The grandfather I never knew about turned into dust. The mother that gave birth to me did, too."

"Blood magic is dangerous. What Reyna did was-"

"What she did was awful, Mom. I know that. I get that. She did it to herself. She could've handled the relationship with her father so differently. But she made the choice she thought was best. It was all she knew to do."

Mom sighed.

"Even with all the things she did to haunt me and he did to get my attention, I still wish I could have known them better."

Mom nodded.

"I don't know."

Loud talking came from the front of the apartment. I looked to the closed bedroom door. "They're still here?"

Mom stood up and headed to the door. "They are. And when you're ready, breakfast is ready. Come join us." She left the room and closed the door behind her.

I surveyed my mother's room and saw two new pictures on the altar. I got off the bed and kneeled at the altar. One picture displayed Raymond in his prime, dressed in a shiny suit. With Reyna gone, I knew it would be on me to venerate Raymond. If I couldn't know him in this world, I was honored to work with him through the altar.

The other was of Reyna. It was recent and had an inscription on the back. "To my Ruby Imani," I read, "whose love I will never deserve. My love I will always give. Thank you."

I kissed the photo and put it back on the altar. I closed my eyes and focused on my breath, preparing to meditate. I was interrupted by a large commotion in the living room. I ran down the long hallway, my heart racing with concern.

"What's wrong? What's going on?" My heart beat loudly as I observed Teddy, Loreen, Dr. Pike, Gabriel and Mom in a commotion near the door. Each one was talking over the other.

"Mom! What is going on?" I yelled over the din. Everyone ceased speaking and spread away. In the center stood Keisha, her smile wide and bright.

"Keisha!" I rushed to my friend. "What are you doing here? How...how did you get in Tiwa?" We embraced.

"I heard about the borders and headed here as soon as I could," Keisha replied, reluctantly letting go.

"The Prayer Helpers," Mom mumbled in a somber tone. "The Prayer Helpers are gone."

"What?" I glanced around the room. "The Prayer Helpers are gone? What does that mean?"

Teddy walked forward with his fists clenched tightly at his side. "The boundary into Tiwa has been breached, Imani."

"And history, once again, most certainly repeats itself," Dr. Pike added, almost resignedly.

Acknowledgements

Thank you to my wonderful beta readers, Kristi, Lachysha, and Solomon. Your feedback was invaluable and kept me on the path to completing the book.

Thank you to my editors, Lori and Ebony, for seeing the vision and helping me get there.

Thank you to my book designers, E.L. and Daniel for creating covers that capture Imani and Yardley House.

Finally, thanks to Lachysha for pushing me to write my first book. You believed in me all these years and I finally listened. Thank you.

Author's Note

Thank you for your sharing in my first novel, Imani's Heart: Book One in the Tiwa Series. The journey from an idea to a book took early morning writing sessions and weekend afternoons to bring to fruition. The hours spent in writing classes, write-ins, editing, and re-editing make this first novel of mine really feel like my baby. The isolated time away from my family and work provided me with a catharsis. Learning the characters and understanding the operation of Tiwa taught me about myself in many ways. I hope that you were able to experience some emotions while joining Imani on her journey.

I hope the land of Tiwa has intrigued you to want to know more. The series will delve more into the land and other characters that inhabit it so that the concept of having our own can better be explored. While book two is still in development, I can gladly share that it will take place in the Land of Yipada, a town that thrives upon the water. While those in power determine how to best fix the borders of Tiwa, characters from the mainland and Tiwa have their own challenges to solve.

A review of my work would be the cherry on top of this whole experience. Please take a moment and go to your favorite review site and share your experience with Imani's Heart. I appreciate you both reading and sharing my first book baby.

Sign up for my mailing list to find out what's next in Tiwa at JoyiaManon.com. I'm also on Instagram: @JManonWriting.

Love,
Joyia Manón